Dealers

'Lennox Mayhew.' The BZW dealer's voice was strained.

'Daniel. What's your price in US bonds – thirty year?'

Lennox sounded surprised. 'What do you want with thirty-year Yankee paper?'

'What's your *price*?' Daniel hissed.

'Ninety-six.'

'I'll take fifty.'

'You got fifty.' Lennox tone suggested mild insanity in the caller.

Daniel put down the receiver and took a deep breath. He had just surpassed his personal trading capacity by some twenty million dollars. Now he was in clear space – free flying; if this one didn't work out, an awful lot of money, a good part of the bank itself and, least of all, his own job would go merrily down the drain.

He was completely, terrifyingly alone in unknown territory.

Then he thought again and realized that was not quite right.

Tony Eisner had been here before him.

By the same author
available in Thames Mandarin

Comfort and Joy
The Courier
Sid and Nancy

GERALD COLE

Dealers

From the screenplay by
ANDREW MACLEAR

Thames Mandarin

A Thames Mandarin Paperback

DEALERS

First published in Great Britain 1989
by Mandarin Paperbacks
Michelin House, 81 Fulham Road, London SW3 6RB
in association with
Thames Television International Ltd
149 Tottenham Court Road, London S1P 9LL

Mandarin is an imprint of the Octopus Publishing Group

British Library Cataloguing in Publication Data

Cole, Gerald
  Dealers.
  I. Title
  813′.54 [F]

  ISBN 0-7493-0057-4

Printed and bound in Great Britain
by Cox and Wyman Ltd,
Reading, Berks

One

On the morning of his death Tony Eisner rose at five fifteen, showered, dressed, then shaved, standing at the broad, arched, living room window of his Bermondsey three-bedroom pied-à-terre. Dawn gilded the grey waters of the Thames two storeys below.

He had slept for just four hours – courtesy of an early hiccup on the Tokyo market he had monitored on his bedside VDU. But fatigue was only visible in a faint shadowing along the broad, well-groomed planes of his cheeks. His eyes were clear, his breath newly minted.

He was a short, compact man in his mid-thirties, though two minutes in his presence dispelled any awareness of diminished stature. Dynamism oozed from every pore, overruling more conventional social indicators like his Eton-Oxford veneer, or the tastefully expensive cut of his clothing.

It showed now as he placed his electric razor on the sill and turned to glance quickly across the flat. Interior designed in minimalist hi-tech, its impersonal gloss was marred only by Eisner's weekday bachelorhood untidiness. His girlfriend would occasionally reposition the odd cushion or print-out. His wife, on rare excursions from their six-bedroom Hampshire home, refused to touch a thing.

Eisner's expression registered satisfaction. He had bought the flat on the proceeds of a Eurobond killing at the start of the docklands boom. Even in today's property doldrums he would clear a cool hundred thousand profit.

Draining the warmed-over dregs of last night's coffee, he packed a slim, black document case, activated the flat's security system and took the lift to the basement car park. Five minutes later his late registration seven series BMW was gliding across a Tower Bridge already dotted with commercial traffic.

Half a mile northward, at the heart of the City, the narrow streets were clear. The head office of the Whitney Paine investment bank – Eisner's destination – elbowed its way eight storeys skyward at the junction of New and Old Broad Streets. Its fluted aluminium facade mimicked that of the Nat West Tower barely five hundred yards away; by coincidence, claimed Whitney Paine's directors: by presumption, said the rest of the City.

An alleyway off New Broad Street gave access to a large underground car park. Eisner entered the bank's entrance lobby via a narrow, concrete staircase. An elderly security guard, not expecting the early morning rush for a good hour yet, jerked awake behind the reception console. Nodding curtly, Eisner mounted the steel-sided escalator that rose, humming softly, to the first floor.

Yawning, a uniformed cleaner pushed an electric polisher across the broad, marbled expanse of the main hall. Ignored, Eisner moved briskly to the trading floor door, tapped out the entrance code and slipped inside.

It was a large, high-ceilinged room at the corner of the building, tall windows on two sides spilling early light onto the broken octagon of the dealing desks and their banks of blank-screened VDUs.

The untypical emptiness and silence of the room made even Eisner pause.

For twelve hours a day this was the hub of the bank's market-making activities. Twenty dealers – backed by assistants, clerks, analysts, supernumeraries – sat hunched over keyboards, transfixed by flickering green and multi-coloured columns, wheedling, pleading, yelling into a gorgon-tangle of competing telephones; a barely restrained bedlam in unrelenting pursuit of profit. One blink, it seemed, and the entire circus would be restored. Eisner did not blink. He did not need to. The circus had been running in his head, day in, day out, for the past five years. For the past three months it had not even paused for sleep.

He moved across the grey-carpeted floor to his own desk: the dollar desk. Clean now, empty, like all the positions in its immediate vicinity: Elana Cimino on domestic corporate sales: Wolfgang Bauer heading up currency deals: Daniel Pascoe juggling the Far East. *We few, we happy few, we band of brothers*. The crème de la crème. And a small grin for Daniel – 'the grammar school oick'; an old jibe, treading on his heels for as long as he had been here.

Not any more.

But he wouldn't think of that.

He wouldn't think of any of them.

He walked back through the octagon and re-emerged into the main hall. He took the lift to the eighth floor.

The boardroom faced north, the pale light from its picture window lost in the dark wood panelling. Eisner did not switch on the lights. For the first time since rising he showed signs of weariness. Moving to the head of the long table that dominated the room, he placed his case on the polished walnut and sat, heavily.

There was, he realized, never a moment's total silence in this place. Heating elements clicked, the building fabric shifted and stirred minutely: beyond, there was the low rumble of the City – slight at this hour, but there if you paused to listen: and, more tenuous but no less real, the electric pulse of the money market itself; slackening off in the Far East now, but racing ever closer across the surface of the planet in an undisciplined ecstasy of activity, both human and electronic.

The market had been good to him, a brutal task-master but a bounteous one, more bounteous than he had dared dream when he had first entered it thirteen years ago. And now, he found, more brutal than he had really believed possible.

But he would not complain. A good trader never admitted defeat or regret, and he was a lot better than good.

He breathed in; he had not felt so sure, so positive, so clear-minded for months. Then he snapped open the locks of his document case, lifted the lid and looked inside. The temptation to switch on the Quotron that lay there was a sourness at the edge of his thinking, easily dismissed as nonsense. Nothing could be changed now.

Instead he picked up the sleek, black Heckler and Koch automatic next to it and slipped off the safety catch.

The sudden wild beating of his heart, the prickling of sweat in his armpits, disturbed him. Quickly he reversed the slim weapon, propped its short barrel against his lower teeth and closed his mouth over the black metal.

He had bought the weapon, and a single clip of ammunition, in a Soho pub two weeks earlier. It had cost him a thousand pounds, his cheapest capital bid of the day.

But, as he discovered when he squeezed, rather than jerked, the neat trigger – exactly as its nervous vendor had instructed him – it did its job perfectly well.

Two

Daniel Pascoe's Cessna 180 seaplane came unstuck at fifty knots and bucked into the clear Kentish sky. It cleared the head of an irate combine harvester driver by a good sixty feet.

Prop roar cancelled by the thunder of U2's *Passion* on four-speaker CD, the single-engined aircraft climbed through a slow turn, circling back on the converted oast house, with adjoining lake, that was Daniel's home. At twelve hundred feet he eased back on the control column and levelled off, muting the CD while he called for a weather report from Biggin Hill Air Traffic Control.

A swift glance through the cabin window showed him the chequerboard wheatlands and orchards of the High Weald, crystal clear in the early morning sunshine. Then he was thumbing at the laptop lying across his knees. The rows of green figures tumbling down the narrow VDU were bond prices on the Tokyo Stock Exchange. The weather report arrived, and he gave his height and course before signing off, eyes still fixed on Tokyo.

'Hotel India out. Thank you.'

Broad forehead puckering, he was already reaching for the mobile phone built into the instrument panel. He punched a memory button.

'Whitney Paine. Dunbar here.'

The voice in Daniel's ear was transatlantic, high-pitched, flustered.

'Jamie?' Daniel snapped. 'What's with these gyrations in the long bond?'

'Never mind that,' the voice cried. 'You better get in here fast. Eisner shot himself – couple of hours ago. The place is going crazy!'

'What!'

Turbulence struck the plane from nowhere, dropping it a dozen feet and slewing it sideways. Stunned, Daniel steadied the control column. But the laptop had already slid off his knees and bumped to the floor.

They had been alike as two peas growing from different ends of the same pod. While Eisner had been Oxbridge smooth, Pascoe was redbrick rough.

They had entered the City fray within two years of each other, first clashing in their mid-twenties as half-commission men on the old Stock Exchange floor. Their flamboyant styles had ruffled feathers almost as much as their tendency to guess right.

The flamboyance had drawn them together, if only in similar views of their world. To both, the market had been a game; the best, most exhilarating game in town. A daily emotional rollercoaster, headier than any artificial drug, with a regular shakeout of over-priced trinkets that brought Christmas with every killing.

'It's not the money that counts, Danny boy,' Tony had once told him, half cut on Bollinger and halfway through a fencing match with Havana Coronas, 'it's the *fun*.'

But in the last three months at Whitney Paine – bastion of Wall Street and Big Bang predator of the City – there had been precious little of that.

★ ★ ★

At seven ten the Cessna touched down in the Pool of London. Taxiing within five hundred yards of Tony Eisner's riverside flat, into which at that moment a posse of fraud-minded CID were attempting to break and enter, Daniel circled before Tower Bridge and bumped to a halt at a private jetty close by Alderman Stairs. At seven twenty-five, having paused only to snatch twenty Marlborough from a tube kiosk, he was sidestepping rush hour crowds outside the Whitney Paine building. In the lobby a uniformed constable talked to a wan-faced security guard, who repeatedly shook his head.

Frowning, Daniel mounted the escalator. In the main hall signs of alarm and confusion were more obvious. Staff milled about, hanging expectantly in doorways, or huddling in watchful groups. Near the lifts a slim, dark-haired girl sobbed discreetly, comforted by a friend. Not even Black Monday had had that effect.

Reaching for a cigarette, Daniel felt his elbow jogged. He turned to catch the swift flash of interest in the glance of a petite blonde girl, aged about twenty-five and pretty; she bustled past him, flanked by two scruffily dressed individuals bearing video equipment. TV already. There had been nothing on the radio before he had landed, not even LBC. *Always go for the big splash, Tony.* The thought struck him instantly as cheap.

Loud voices came from the dealing room as its door opened and shut. But the door before it was also ajar.

Daniel ducked his head inside.

The office was medium-sized, dominated by its glass-wall view of the trading floor next door. A broad, well-built man stood against it, hunched shoulders stretching the expensive grey worsted of his Huntsman suit. He turned as Daniel entered and nodded, picking a ready-clipped cigar off his desk and lighting it with the two-inch stub of the one he already held.

'What the hell happened?' asked Daniel.

Robbie Barrell's wide, finely seamed face looked haggard. In six years Daniel had never seen the senior trader looking every one of his forty-eight years, and more.

'Eisner shot himself. Right here in the boardroom.'

Barrell's East End vowels were thicker than his tobacco-clogged vocal cords could justify. He stared hard at Daniel, as if he expected to be contradicted.

Daniel could think of nothing to say. Death wasn't part of the game he knew. Nowadays no one *killed themselves* just because they cocked up. That was incomprehensible; that was obscene.

Sighing, Robbie collapsed into his desk chair. 'Jesus Christ – I've got to tell his wife. Tell me how I'm going to do that?'

The trilling intercom saved Daniel from an impossible reply. Robbie snatched up the receiver, listened, then pushed it down again. 'Come on, upstairs. Mallory wants a word.' Grim-faced, he heaved himself out of his chair.

Daniel shrugged in disbelief. 'I was speaking to Tony six hours ago – '

'Damn!' Robbie interrupted, grinding his freshly lit cigar into an ashtray. 'I feel responsible. I should've seen this coming.'

'We're all under pressure for Chrissakes – '

Robbie's gaze hardened. 'Tony was under one hundred million bucks' worth.'

So he was over-stretched. He always came back before.

But Barrell was already halfway through the door. Beyond the window heads turned, noting his departure.

Daniel hurried after him into the main hall, just as figures spilled from the dealing room.

'Robbie, have you had any word from upstairs . . . ?'

'I'm going there now.'

'Mr Barrell, do we open as normal . . . ?'

'Course we bloody do.'

Daniel stayed level as Barrell accelerated, trying to outpace a growing entourage.

The older man swore under his breath. 'All hell's going to break loose upstairs. And the press'll turn it into a circus – you watch. What a bloody mess . . .' The lift doors opened as he reached them.

'Robbie.' a girl clerk asked, 'who'll be running the dollar book?'

Involuntarily Daniel's eyes flickered towards Barrell for his reaction. The senior trader's face was a preoccupied mask. As the lift doors closed, Daniel jumped in beside him.

I can run the dollar book. I can do anything Eisner could – and better. It's got to come to me.

But, as the lift rose silently, he could find no way of speaking his thoughts.

And yet – from whatever cause – the bank's principal trading desk remained on offer.

The boardroom was full of sunlight. As he followed Robbie through the door, Daniel saw an upturned chair at the head of the long table. Adjoining it white tape outlined the form of a body. Dark, surprisingly sparse stains spotted the carpet.

Then Daniel's angle of vision changed and he realized that a massive crescent, spreading from the chair's position across almost the full width of the table, was not some blemish in the polished surface but blood.

'*Shit*,' he breathed.

Pausing at the head of the table, Robbie seemed mesmerized by the same stark image.

Two nondescript men fussed with tiny brushes at the window blinds. Next to them, gazing out across the City, stood the stiff, greying figure of Frank Mallory.

As the door clicked shut, the bank's senior British director turned and inclined his head briefly towards Barrell. If he saw Daniel, he made no sign.

'This is a bad one, Robbie.'

Barrell sucked in breath, fumbled in an inside pocket for a new cigar. 'Jesus,' he murmured, flicking twice at his lighter, even though it flared the first time. 'How do I tell his wife? I have to do that now.'

Daniel registered the slight tremor in the senior trader's hand, as he was sure Mallory did, too. Robbie's fondness for Scotch – strictly out of office hours – was a discreet legend, though Daniel had never seen it impair the man's judgement.

But, for once, the director seemed understanding. 'I know,' he said, moving towards the table. 'We have to do that right away; but there's another problem right behind that one.'

'What's that?' Daniel cut in.

The faintest flicker of annoyance in Mallory's glance included Daniel for the first time. 'This may sound indelicate,' the director said, 'but having your dollar trader lose one hundred million in a quarter and then blow his brains out all over your boardroom table – ' He paused, focussing on Barrell. 'It's not the most positive signal you can send your shareholders. There's going to be a lot of pressure on all of us, particularly you, Robbie.'

Barrell sucked at his cigar. It was not something he needed to be reminded of. 'In ten minutes I've got a research call,' he said quickly. 'I'll switch Daniel from gilts to the dollar book.'

Got it. Daniel's heart bumped; he was actually turning towards the door when he saw Mallory's finely chiselled lips tighten in a moue of disapproval.

'That won't work, Robby. Whatever we do now is going to be scrutinized with a laser beam. I can't recommend that we put Daniel in charge of the dollar book.'

'Why not?' Daniel snapped.

Both Barrell and Mallory were looking at him now, Barrell with evident surprise, Mallory with a narrowing gaze that held ill-concealed dislike. 'You're too damned high-profile, Pascoe,' he said sharply. 'Too damned risky. I can't put you in Eisner's position. The board already think you have a trading style that's too flamboyant. What they mean is it's downright reckless.' The man all but sniffed. 'I won't even recommend you.'

Daniel stared in disbelief. 'You've got a one hundred *million* dollar loss! Who the hell else is going to pull you out of that?'

The outburst seemed to reassure the director. His tone grew more even. 'We have to assume a safe, orthodox position for a while. The only way this hangs together is in a *team* operation, Daniel. This is a respected financial institution, not a damn casino.'

Supercilious bastard!

The thought was clear on Daniel's features. He knew why Mallory was after him. The man was the last survivor of Hobson Fellowes, the small, discreet, highly respected merchant bank Whitney Paine had swallowed whole to get its City foothold – an old-style city man, cushioned by old school ties and a private income; self-assured, suave and bloody treacherous.

He had tolerated Eisner because they shared a background, and Eisner added noughts to the bank's assets – until three months ago. Now Daniel, who had Eisner's flair but nothing of his class, could act the scapegoat, suffer for his ungentlemanly presumption. And Mallory would keep sweet with his Wall Street masters.

'Look – ' Daniel began, and caught the warning light in Barrell's eyes.

'I'll get Patrick Skill to cover,' the senior trader said.

Daniel entered the trading floor in a fuming fug. Nothing of what Mallory had said made sense. Safety first, teamwork wouldn't solve a thing. This game was about risk; the hairier the better. That came down to one man making a calculated decision, having the balls to follow it through.

Or one woman.

Entering the hubbub, he caught Elana Cimino's eye as she swivelled at her domestic corporate sales desk. Shock-haired and plumpish, an ebullient twenty-three year old, she gave him an uncharacteristically fragile smile.

'I'm really sorry about Tony,' she said, catching his arm as he passed.

Daniel nodded, touched; in his anger he had almost forgotten he and Tony were supposed to have been friends.

Jamie Dunbar, Daniel's assistant, appeared at his elbow. 'Daniel, here's that long bond update you wanted.'

As Daniel took a scrap of telex, Robbie Barrell, arriving at his usual position at the long edge of the octagon, called the room to attention. The babble of conversation died quickly. This was the daily research call, a combination of market assessment, strategy meeting for the day's trading and pep talk. After the morning's events, the latter had the highest priority.

Barrell straightened, planting his hands firmly on his desk top. However painful his call to Eisner's wife, it seemed to have exorcized something. To Daniel's eye, the senior trader's jitters had gone, replaced by something steadier, more thoughtful, more the Robbie he knew. Above Barrell's head the middle of three large clocks registered eight a.m. The two either side marked Tokyo and New York time.

'I want to say something about pressure.' Barrell paused, his eyes scanning the room as he let the words sink in. 'I want you all to remember that this business is like a carousel. What goes around, comes around. And I want you to remember that however black things can look, a new day always dawns. And at the end of the day, this is a business. It isn't your whole life.'

Tell that to Tony Eisner. Daniel's gaze intersected with Barrell's.

Barrell drew in breath. 'What happened here this morning is terrible. No one can feel worse than I do. But we *have* to put that aside for now.'

He paused again, searching the faces turned to him. It was, Daniel realized suddenly, the only funeral oration Eisner would be receiving in this company.

'Let me talk about the dollars for today – ' Barrell's tone was immediately brisk, business-like. A smoking cigar, out of sight until now, appeared in his hand. 'In the foreign exchange, currencies are still bid; it's not feeding through in any more Jap buying. They're all waiting on the trades.

I don't see any reason to change our basic bear tack.' He glanced over at Daniel. 'What about the gilts?'

'I've covered the shorts in Tokyo,' Daniel told him. 'I reckon that's the way we should be going. Let's look for a better level to sell. That goes for currencies as well.'

As Barrell nodded, Elana Cimino broke in. 'Particularly the long end.'

Barrell looked at the chief currency trader, the tall, lean West German with the chiselled features of a cigar store Indian. 'Wolfgang?'

'There's been some buying in marks, but it's domestic, eight to nine years.' Wolfgang Bauer's accent was crisply Teutonic, a rich source for Elana Cimino's talent for mimicry. 'Looks technical,' he continued. 'My man in the sand's buying too. I'm going to run with it.' He raised an encouraging eyebrow. 'We're long two hundred and fifty million.'

Barrell sent a plume of cigar smoke ceilingward. 'Your man in the sand . . .' On any other day he might have smiled. Wolfgang's Gulf contacts were legendary, and much prized; they had helped him make the leap from the bank's Frankfurt subsidiary.

'Denmark's still political,' Elana Cimino noted. 'I think the agricultural spending package will go through.'

'We're still short oh four oh eight's,' Jamie Dunbar added. 'But the currency should bail us out.'

Barrell nodded again. The pall thrown over the room by Eisner hung heavy; he could smell it; like fear, like greed – those twin motors of the market – but more insidious, more destructive. It would take days, weeks, to dispel it. He could do no more for now. The market would have to do his work for him.

'OK,' he announced. 'Deep breaths everyone; plenty of oxygen. Keep your heads. Let's get to it.'

The hubbub resumed. Daniel dropped into his seat next to Jamie Dunbar, eyes fastening on the Reuters screen between them. It showed figures from Tokyo. Dimly at his back we was aware of Elana's voice rising. 'I don't want junk bonds, Carl. You're just *wrong* about this market. But put a circle round those marks for me – September's. Right.' A querulous grunt. 'What? No, I'm busy tonight . . .'

Attention back on his screen, Daniel picked up his phone and pressed a tab on the board in front of him. On the far side of the room a salesman's phone flashed. Daniel spoke softly: 'What happened with your twenty million buyer?' He sniffed as he got his answer. 'Just prospecting, eh?'

He cut the connection and slumped in his chair, glancing idly round the octagon. Sometimes it wasn't always wise for the left hand to know what the right was doing.

A tab flashed in front of him. Jamie Dunbar leaned over. 'Jimmy Kelly on forty-three.'

Daniel shook his head. Let things stew for the moment.

Another tab blinked immediately. 'Max Borisoff,' said Jamie.

Daniel grimaced and waved him away.

A third tab came alive. 'O'Halloran at Manny Hanny.'

'No.'

'You going to talk to anyone today?' Jamie's youthful, aquiline features creased in exasperation; sometimes he thought Daniel acted this way just to wind him up. Yet another tab flashed. Jamie glanced at his board. 'Lennox,' he said.

'Yeah.' Daniel jerked upright, snapping out of his apparent lethargy. 'I'll talk to Lennox.' He picked up his phone, pressed the tab and listened. 'Winnies – thirty-five, thirty-seven. In what size?' He smiled briefly, hearing the suppressed eagerness in Lennox Mayhew's voice, seeing the dealer's lean, rangy form crouch forward over his desk at BZW barely half a mile away. 'Your size, sir. Fifty I sell you. Talk to you.' He cut the connection and turned to Jamie. 'Fifty million, out to Lennox.'

Jamie nodded and scribbled a note as Daniel lit a cigarette. A ten-second call had just earned the bank fifteen thousand profit, minus Daniel's commission.

From behind he heard Elana consulting the in-house lunch menu. 'Hey, Wolfgang, what's your position on lunch?'

'Just a sandwich,' came the German's clipped tones.

'OK. Ham and cheese. You want a beer?'

'I'll take a mineral water.'

There was a hiccup of laughter from Elana, which made Daniel smile.

'Wolfgang . . . it's, you know? I love it. All this *control*.'

Daniel turned to catch Wolfgang's quizzical glance over the top of his desk.

Elana, sitting across from him, shuddered theatrically. 'It just makes me feel weird, you know?'

Wolfgang's expression was calculatedly deadpan. 'I like to be in control,' he enunciated carefully.

Elana manufactured a gasping swoon across the desktop, and abruptly sprang up again. 'Hey, Wolfgang!' she purred brightly. 'I think you should take the price sticker off that Porsche you got.'

Jamie caught Daniel's eye and snickered. The Elana-Wolfgang contest was standard dealing room entertainment; it was difficult to know which of them enjoyed it more – and how far it extended beyond office hours.

Daniel glanced back at his VDU to see figures changing. Three tabs flashed simultaneously on his board: Movement at last. But, as he picked up his phone again, his gaze snagged on the empty chair two desks away: the dollar desk.

Waste, he thought. *Bloody waste*.

Though of what, and of whom, he had no time to elaborate, even to himself.

Three

Heavy paws thumped onto Daniel's chest, followed by a malodorous blast of canine breath. He shuddered upright in the darkened room, grunting in alarm as a large, wet tongue slapped his cheek. A heavy, dark-furred head swung towards the digital clock beside the bed. 'Three o'clock!' He frowned at the wolfhound, which cocked its head quizzically. 'What's the matter with you? You always wake me at twelve on Saturday. That's the arrangement, damn it!'

The dog bridled and unrolled its tongue.

Sighing, unfussed, Daniel ruffled its head, then threw back the duvet, forcing the animal to scramble back off the bed.

A jam swallowed his taxi whole in Soho Square, so he paid up and strolled the rest of the way, belatedly relishing the opportunity of exercise.

After fourteen years in the City, there was still a sense of release in swapping business suit and tie – even though, jointly they ran into four figures – for leather jacket, T-shirt, jeans and loafers. He half wished Bonnie had chosen somewhere smarter to meet, somewhere that would look askance at the casual attire, so that he could point out the Armani jeans and T-shirt, the leather jacket hand-stitched in Florence, the hundred-and-twenty-pound Timberland footwear. Arsehole dreams, he knew, but sweet ones; and he needed something sweet to happen after a week like the last.

At eight fifteen Kettner's was nearly full. Daniel picked his way through the bamboo chairs, the low tables and the crush, and saw Bonnie, perched on a stool at the far end of the bar. By dint of a steely smile – quite at odds with her fey, softly pretty looks – she had contrived to keep a second stool to herself.

Daniel slid onto it without a word, beckoned the bar tender and kissed the petite brunette gently on the lips. When they disengaged, the bar tender was there.

'Another of those, and a Scotch on the rocks,' Bonnie said, pushing her empty glass across the bar.

'And make it,' Daniel added gruffly, 'unusually large.' He watched as Bonnie gave him a quietly welcoming smile – he was, after all, only ten minutes late – and took a Marlborough from a packet on the bar top.

Her loose curls framed doe eyes, a discreetly upturned nose; her prettiness had a vulnerability which reassured him. She looked like a daughter of the middle classes, slightly adrift; which at this point in her life was not wholly inaccurate.

When her cigarette was alight, he eased it out of her fingers. As she lit another, he inhaled deeply and glanced around the bar. 'The market's killing me,' he announced. 'It's all over the place.'

Bonnie's face fell. Her relationship with Daniel had never been even – that was part of its appeal – but tonight she felt particularly fragile.

'Daniel, I know,' she warned. 'But could we leave it behind for this evening?' He blinked as she moved closer, her eyes softening as she hooked an arm through his. 'Remember the first time we came here?'

Their drinks appeared in front of them. Daniel reached for his, only to pause, gazing into the amber liquid. 'Last night,' he said, 'I dreamt I was in the boardroom with Tony. The gun was on the table. Robbie Barrell was standing there. Tony asked him to do it. Robbie told him not to be crazy. Then Tony asked me instead. And then – '

'What?'

'He just did it right in front of us.'

In the hiatus that followed, Bonnie's sigh was the faintest exhalation of breath. She turned to draw at her cigarette. Daniel shook his head. Talking to Bonnie always clarified things for him; as usual, he had forgotten until he actually saw her.

'At first it didn't seem to touch me. But now – ' He glanced up, suddenly aware that he had lost her attention. 'You want to eat?'

'Sure.' She stubbed out her cigarette, eyes still down.

Daniel frowned. 'What's wrong?'

'Nothing's wrong.' She gave him a swift, warm smile, eased off her stool and tugged at his arm. 'Come on – let's go.'

He entered her with a fierceness that verged on aggression, jerking a sharp cry from her as he pulled her slim thighs back onto his. To him their coupling seemed a balletic act, startling them both in its energy and precision: their lust was something apart from them, a third force that possessed and invigorated, transforming them into awed spectators of their own intensity, until the release of orgasm.

In the thirteen months they had been together, Daniel had only been aware of the sex getting better and better.

Exhausted, beaded with sweat, he nuzzled gratefully

against her shoulder, breaking suddenly into a slow chuckle.

'Can't we do this for a living?'

Bonnie stirred under him. 'I don't have the stamina.'

He chuckled again, letting his chin savour the soft weight of her breast.

After a moment she shuddered. 'I can't stop shaking.'

He felt the same tremor – a rippling but pleasurable unease, born out of sex, but extending further, deeper. He had barely glimpsed it before her.

'I do love you, Bonnie,' he said suddenly.

He was surprised by her equally sudden silence.

'You love *me*,' she said after a long moment, 'or you love fucking me?'

Her voice shocked him with its distance.

Sitting opposite her in the bath, he watched the foam cluster about her breasts, all but masking the pink stubs of her nipples. They were not enormous breasts by cup-size, but her narrow back and the warm water that buoyed them up exaggerated their roundness and fullness. It was easier to register their erotic effect, even if he was too tired to do anything about it, than examine the suddenly complicated emotional situation.

Close emotions disturbed him. He knew *he* was unreasonable, demanding, unreliable – up when the market was up, down when a deal crashed. He knew he dumped most of it on her. But she had never complained; her very calmness invited the confidences. Her own upsets were quiet sulks, moments of retreat that seemed to run their course and fade away on their own. Daniel had handled them by simply ignoring them, or retreating himself until a better time. But as he looked up into her eyes, hoping for warmth or irony, anything but the steady, coolly appraising gaze he got, he realized this time was going to be different.

Love, he thought. Mentioning love had upset the balance. Out of long ingrained caution, he had been careful never to use the word before.

Without warning, she stood up and stepped out of the bath. Pulling a towel from the rail, she wrapped it around herself and went out, not looking back. The door swung shut. In a moment ice cubes tinkled distantly into a glass.

Daniel stared at the dissolving foam where Bonnie had lain. Compared to intimate relationships, the uncertainties of the market were a doddle. He loathed not being able to judge the odds. If there was going to be an explosion he wanted it now. Quickly.

It came near the bottom of a bottle of J & B.

Slumped on the sofa, she set her glass down on the arm and eyed him down the length of her body. 'I can't go on with this any longer,' she said, without a trace of drunkenness.

They had been laughing for a while, sliding towards the end of the evening, and for a moment he had thought her mood might have improved. But he obviously wasn't going to be reprieved.

'What?' he said warily. 'Us?' He was curled in the armchair opposite her, his knees up.

'Right,' she said. 'I can't do it. I mean . . . it isn't anything.' She gestured exaggeratedly, showing how much she had drunk, but her voice was still steady. 'All we do is drink and screw and then drink again.'

Daniel swung his legs down, picked the bottle off the carpet and topped up his glass. 'What's wrong with that?'

His grin seemed to shatter her calm. 'For one thing,' she snapped, 'I'm turning into an *alcoholic*. That's what!'

Sitting up, she reached for her glass, and immediately slapped it down again. 'See? *Jesus!*' She took a deep breath. 'I want a relationship with someone . . . you . . . but all you can think about is the damn bank and some deal and I'm just like a narcotic you use. We just stew ourselves in booze and then fuck each other's brains out, and then you get in your plane and fly off! Does that constitute a *relationship* in your mind?' She stared at him, wonderingly, genuinely puzzled.

Daniel looked back. He had never seen her so determined, so forceful. 'Well,' he said uneasily, 'I thought it was – the arrangement was – '

'An *arrangement*,' Bonnie cut across him, nodding with a kind of exaggerated thoughtfulness. 'That's a better word . . . We have an arrangement . . .'

Daniel echoed her nod, grabbing at straws. 'That we maintained our independence.'

Bonnie gave a gasp of disbelief. 'I don't *want* to have an arrangement,' she cried. 'I don't want to feel independent. I want to feel *safe!*' She shook her head, as though trying to free it of cobwebs. 'I don't think I can carry on dealing with your moods and your crises and people blowing their brains out in your office. It's like nothing is real – '

Her emotions seemed to reach such a pitch she could no longer articulate them. Instead she snatched at a cigarette, lit it and inhaled deeply, staring past him.

Daniel waited, treading water, knowing that any word was likely to be the wrong one. 'Do you want me to go?' he said at last.

'Yes. No!'

Now she looked at him, and tears welled. The force had vanished as swiftly and as disturbingly as it had come. 'I want this to be different, that's all. I just want us to be like everyone else, come home and have dinner . . . see a film, and now and again go to sleep sober. Is that a lot to ask, Daniel?'

He wanted to shake his head, but the gesture seemed redundant. Instead he said quietly, 'I suppose not.' Then he took a deep breath, and stood. 'I think I'd better leave.'

Her grunt was dismissive, accusatory once more. 'See? Now you're going to go. What'll I do – sleep with this bottle?' Her foot lashed out, catching the whisky. It spun across the carpet and rolled to a halt against the armchair, empty.

Shaken, Daniel stepped over it.

His hand hung on the front door catch. 'I'll call you tomorrow.' He said it quietly, diffidently, like a peace offering.

'I just wanted it to be different.'

Her tears came in a torrent now, uncontrolled, scalding him. He shut his eyes and stepped outside, squeezing the door shut as though stealth would diminish the effect of his departure.

Love. That's what had done it. everything had been fine, but he had had to put his foot in it.

What in God's name was going wrong with this week?

Shit, he thought.

'Shit!'

Four

'Hit him again,' said Robbie Barrell. 'Once more – '

Fastened to the screen in front of him, his eyes gleamed. The share price marked by a flashing asterisk leapt a point; a voice spoke hurriedly from the telephone at his ear.

'Thirty bid!' Robbie echoed, and chuckled loudly. 'Hit him again!'

One million shares in a major corporation he had bought cheap on rumours of poor quarterly figures – rumours scotched by a press release only ten minutes old – were selling at a rate of knots as the market realized its mistake.

'Luverly!' Robbie roared, his grin wolfish. A final thirty thousand vanished within seconds. 'I'm done.'

Across the trading floor, Daniel, watching from his desk, sent a congratulatory grin. Observing a past master like Robbie in full flow was always an education.

'Thanks, Evan,' Robbie spoke into his telephone. 'Nice doing business. By the way, how's Lucille?' The reply caused his jubilant expression to sag fractionally. 'Evan, I'm sorry – but you always suspected she was a guy, right?' He laughed. 'OK, Evan, be in touch.'

Another busted relationship.

Daniel stamped on the thought ruthlessly. Dealers had wives, and girlfriends, like other people had birthdays; emotional instability went with the job. But he was glad that Tokyo seemed as sluggish as he felt. It had been a weekend he could gladly have postponed for ever.

'Daniel.'

He glanced up and saw Robbie at his side, cigar in mouth, pulling on his jacket.

'We're wanted – upstairs.'

'What's up?' Daniel frowned, rising.

Robbie blew smoke ceilingward. 'Mallory,' he said.

Mallory's office was large, richly carpeted and decorated with hunting prints that, on examination, proved to be exceptionally gory. But as Daniel entered, a step behind Barrell, the murkier depths of Mallory's nature were suddenly the very last thing on his mind.

The heavy figure of Lee Peters, the bank's senior director, loomed against Mallory's desk. Behind it stood Mallory himself. And next to Peters, a slim, blonde, strikingly attractive young woman three or four years Daniel's junior.

As his heart bumped in surprise, Daniel was abruptly aware that her cool, blue-eyed gaze was fixed on him just as intently.

'Robbie, Daniel.' Peters' smile appeared as if by magic; his eyes glittered behind steel-rimmed spectacles that had earned him the soubriquet of 'Himmler' in less exalted regions. 'Thank you for coming up.'

Robbie nodded and reached for a fresh cigar. Peters' transatlantic bonhomie did not impress him.

'Gentlemen – ' still smiling, the American turned to the young woman, 'this is Anna Schumann. Anna was over at Merrill. She's going to be joining us – well, effectively, as of now.'

Daniel and Robbie blinked simultaneously. There was only one vacancy at the bank that would concern them.

Peters confirmed it. 'Anna's going to be running the dollar book.'

The silence that followed seemed to freeze the room. Only Peters appeared unaware of it. 'Frank,' he said, turning to Mallory, 'I'll be in my office later if you need me. Anna – ' he smiled at her again, 'Welcome aboard.' As she thanked him, he moved smoothly to the door. 'Gentlemen – ' He nodded and had gone.

Daniel flashed a glance at Robbie, and started forward.

'Why wasn't I informed, Frank?' Robbie cut in suddenly, pre-empting the young man. 'I think I should have been consulted. This is something we should discuss.'

Mallory's look was both wary and adamant. 'It's *been* discussed. At board level.'

'As chief trader – ' Robbie stiffened; his tone grew stronger, 'I expect to be consulted about the engagement of key personnel. No disrespect to Miss Schuman.' He barely nodded her way. 'My judgement, which is what you hired me for, says that Daniel should take the dollar book. He gets results, Frank: we *need* results.'

Mallory's gaze was unblinking. 'Miss Schumann has an excellent record over at Merrill.'

Daniel looked at her. She wore high heels, a dark, figure-hugging dress, the hemline high enough to show off excellent legs. Her hair was very blonde, pulled back off her face but allowed to fall freely down her neck and over her shoulders. Her returning gaze was impassive. She looked like a million dollars; and coolly confident enough to handle even more.

Robbie broke a strained silence by glancing quickly at Daniel. 'Come on,' he snapped, 'we're wasting our time here.' He spun on his heels.

As Daniel turned to follow, he caught a wry smile on Anna Schumann's lips. It was a look not of sympathy or commiseration or any fellow-feeling, but of unalloyed triumph.

Green figures flickered on the LCD in front of him. 'Bloody yen,' Daniel muttered, snatched at his whisky glass and gulped down the residue. He glanced at his wristwatch in the candlelight that danced across the restaurant table. Just gone nine.

Kettner's was quiet tonight. He had planned on that when he had left his message on Bonnie's answerphone. A low-alcoholic meal; some gentle fence-mending.

She was already fifteen minutes late.

It was beginning to seem that ever since Eisner had died everything had been on the slide: the markets, Bonnie, now even his livelihood itself.

Anna Schumann's parting smile floated to the top of his mind, as it had done a hundred times since this morning. *Jesus Christ*. The very last thing he wanted was a ball-breaker on his tail.

He had spent two hours of his lunch break pouring alcohol down a Merrill Lynch contact in the Jamaica. None of what he had gleaned had improved his mood: she was twenty-eight years old, New York born, ex-Vassar, three years with Merrill's on Wall Street, three years in the City where she had made some nifty moves in the overcrowded gilts market. Generally regarded as a golden girl: bright, efficient, hard. The bimbo image seemed a calculated distraction; disappointed colleagues called her 'the ice queen' – if any of them had been getting into her pants they had kept damn quiet about it.

He swore under his breath, and was forced to manufacture an apologetic smile for the waitress who had appeared at his elbow. His wristwatch read nine twenty. Refusing a further drink, he asked for the bill and made for the phone in the entrance lobby. The voice that answered belonged to Bonnie's new flatmate, a girl Daniel had only met in passing. She sounded surprised as he asked for Bonnie, interrupting him.

'She's gone to *Frankfurt?*' he cried.

Lufthansa's last flight out of Heathrow touched the tarmac at Frankfurt just after one in the morning. Daniel's taxi deposited him at the Frankfurt Hyatt Hotel within twenty minutes. Bonnie had not yet collected her room key. He scribbled a note and went to wait in the lobby bar.

Shared with one other lone drinker and a visibly bored barman, the place lacked almost all the intimacy he had planned for earlier that night. He was acutely aware that he had been wearing the same clothes for nearly twenty hours, and dark stubble shadowed his chin.

Every gambling instinct he had, and which he relied upon daily, told him the odds were stacked against him. But he didn't want to think about that. Something more urgent – and similarly kept from close examination – had brought him here.

The look on Bonnie's face as she appeared in the bar entrance was not encouraging. She seemed tired and drawn. His note was in her hand. He sprang to his feet, forcing a smile as she walked slowly to the bar.

'What are you doing here, Daniel?' Her tone was both wary and disinterested.

'I had to talk to you,' said Daniel quickly, knowing he had to convince instantly or not all. 'Why d'you leave without telling me?' He nodded towards a nearby cubicle. 'Sit down. I'll get you a drink.'

Her breast rose in a sigh. 'I don't want a drink.'

Daniel nodded. A bad move after Saturday. She remained standing, watching him stiffly.

'What are you doing here?' he asked.

'The magazine's doing a spread on contemporary architecture.' She blinked. 'And I wanted time to think.'

'Architecture?' Daniel laughed. 'This is an architectural wasteland!'

'Some people like it, Daniel.' She spoke tiredly.

He was losing this. He tried again. 'Think about what?'

'You and me.' Another, slower blink.

He wasn't going to stop. 'And?'

Now her eyes dropped; she leaned an arm against the bar top. 'It's over, Daniel. I'm sorry.'

An icy spike drove through his stomach, dragging heart, lungs, every internal organ in a sudden downward plunge.

'But why . . . after all we put into it?'

He heard the quaver in his voice and was appalled.

'Think about that, Daniel.' Her eyes lifted again. 'What have we really put into this? A lot of hard drinking, maybe. Some wild times, I know.'

He laughed humourlessly. 'We went to Uruguay!'

'Yes,' Bonnie said flatly, 'I know we went to Uruguay.'

Daniel stared at her. 'You and I are the only two people I know who've been to Uruguay.'

'So what?' Anger flared in her face.

Abashed, Daniel fumbled for a cigarette. They had done it on a long weekend. Twenty-four bloody hours in the air, and *laughing* all the way. 'I don't want this to end,' he said.

'It's finished, Daniel.'

He looked at her sharply. 'Someone else?'

'That isn't relevant.'

'Christ!' He smacked the cigarette down into an ash tray. 'Can't we *talk* about this? There must be . . .' He shook his head, sighed. 'Isn't there a compromise? Think about it again.' He was staring at her hard. This hurt. This hurt so much he wanted to scream.

Bonnie's eyes glistened as she spoke. 'I *have* thought about it. Again and again. It isn't enough for me. And besides that, your work comes before everything. I haven't stopped loving you. I just can't live with that pressure any longer. Even secondhand, it's too much. I need something more stable.'

It was the speech she had meant to make, sober, on Saturday. From the pain in her eyes, Daniel recognized it. How could they share so much pain, he thought, and *not* be close? It was insane.

He swallowed. 'And you've found something more stable?' As he said it, he remembered the English name scrawled above hers in the hotel register. He hadn't even bothered to read it.

'Yes,' she said quietly, 'I have.'

And it was the pity in her face – much more than the misery – which convinced him she meant every word.

Five

An empty can of Diet Coke carved a low trajectory half the length of the octagon and clunked neatly into Wolfgang Bauer's waste bin.

'Hey, Wolfgang!' Elana Cimino cried. 'I'm in the wrong game!'

Leaning forward across his desk, Wolfgang regarded her through slitted eyes.

Elana chuckled. She had a phone draped over one shoulder; another pressed to her ear. 'Forget it, Carl,' she growled suddenly into the nearest. 'That went out with whitewall tyres and crewcuts.' Frowning, she slammed the receiver back onto its cradle.

Watching, Wolfgang grinned.

Daniel sighed and looked away from the interchange, his attention no more engaged by it than it was by Jamie Dunbar's résumé of the Far East market.

'So,' Jamie was saying, 'we pretty much squared the yen position last night; now it's just loose change . . .'

Daniel nodded, making another effort to concentrate. He felt like death. The BA flight he had hopped from Frankfurt had got him to Heathrow just after seven; too late to make the eight o'clock research call. He had cleaned up perfunctorily on the plane, but sleep had been impossible.

A passing figure distracted him again – distracted him as it had a dozen times since his hurried arrival. Anna

Schumann settled into the dollar desk, excellent legs scissoring neatly. She was wearing black today, a more business-like dress, but still a dress rather than a suit. Black, Daniel reflected, always made blondes look good.

She looked as sleek and efficient and downright bloody sexy as he didn't feel. Aware of his scrutiny, she hooked a blonde strand unnecessarily over her ear, taking the opportunity to lift her gaze from her screen and glance his way. A cool, wary glance of interest; or perhaps simple curiosity at his unkempt appearance.

Ballbuster.

At least Eisner had been competition he could swap jokes with, share the odd pint. Someone as sexually charged as this turned it into a whole new ball game.

Ball, indeed . . .

'So what do you want to do?' Jamie asked.

'What do I want to do about what?'

Jamie frowned, realizing Daniel's attention was elsewhere; then he turned, saw where Daniel's gaze still rested, and his expression lightened.

A puff of cigar smoke announced Robbie Barrell's presence. The senior trader placed an arm on Daniel's shoulder. 'You OK, Daniel? You look knackered.'

'Fine.' Daniel straightened, waved a dismissive hand. 'Tired – I'm here.'

Robbie nodded. He didn't give a damn if Daniel gave up shaving for a week and never changed his shirt, but these days he needed Daniel to have a clear head.

It wasn't Robbie's practice to differentiate between his dealers; if he had allowed Daniel and Tony Eisner more freedom than most it was only because they worked most effectively that way. But Anna Schumann's imposition had put his judgement on the line. He had made up his mind he wouldn't complain, and he wouldn't make her unwelcome, but every instinct told him the ground was shifting under his feet. He badly needed results – and preferably from Daniel.

As if he didn't have enough on his plate without this kind of office politicking.

Drawing on his cigar, he glanced at the wall clock: eight fifty-five. The morning panic was reaching a plateau. A little help wouldn't go amiss.

He moved to the trading floor door, went out into the main hall and slipped into the men's room. Selecting the first empty cubicle, he locked the door, put down the seat lid and sat. The white powder was in a small, clear plastic envelope in the back pocket of his suit trousers. Carefully he laid a thin trail, no more than two inches long, along one palm. Then he raised the palm to his nose, and, blocking one nostril, inhaled sharply through the other.

As the numbness spread through his nasal tissues, he licked the remaining cocaine grains off his hand and replaced the plastic envelope. Just enough left for a mid-afternoon blast before New York opened.

Until recently his indulgence had been slight, and mainly for pleasure. But this past year had been a killer. He couldn't afford to lose his edge.

Splashing his face in cold water at the wash basin, he felt the drug enhance the shock effect. He would slacken off when the dollar book was straight; when the pressure had eased a little.

He peered at his dark-rimmed eyes in the room's wall-length mirror and made himself a solemn promise.

Daniel straightened in his chair, old instincts stirring. 'Could be interested,' he said non-committally into the phone, at the same time gesturing at Jamie to pick up his own receiver and listen in. 'Yeah,' Daniel went on, 'we'll have a look at it. Hey, thanks.' He cut the line and glanced up at Jamie. 'Lennox is looking for a big stake in the five year. Hundred million. Let's fill it.'

Putting down his phone, Jamie looked uneasy. 'Should we do that?'

'Come on, come on!' Daniel snapped. 'Small increments, five, ten million, don't start a panic – '

'But we've got employment figures at two. Shouldn't we wait?'

'Do it!' Daniel cried. 'He's short and he's caught – come *on*!'

Frowning, Jamie picked up his phone again. 'I don't like this.'

Daniel sprang up from his chair. Sucking his teeth, he began to pace the length of the octagon, glancing once, twice, three times at the wall clock. One fifty-two, one fifty-three . . .

Adrenalin pumped through jaded veins; the surface of his mind sparked. He thumped back into his chair, staring at the five-year gilt price on his screen. Just over the mid-nineties; selling even at a one thirty-second rise would give a hefty profit on the numbers Lennox wanted. He would push for a quarter; room to bargain.

'Twenty bought,' Jamie announced.

'Keep going,' Daniel murmured, not lifting his eyes.

He shunted his chair to the Reuters screen between his desk and Jamie's. He punched up a page marked 'Long term indicators', then another reading 'Third quarter employment figures'.

The screen showed one fifty-seven.

He glanced up at Jamie, who nodded. 'They're in place,'

said the young American. Sighing heavily, he threw down his phone and slumped back in his chair.

Daniel swung back towards his own desk and snatched up the phone, pressing a tab. 'Lennox? I'll fill that order for you.'

'What's your price?' asked the BZW dealer.

'Ninety-six and a quarter.'

The Reuters screen changed; now it read, 'Long term indicators combine to depress market. Employment figures below expectations'.

Reaching out, Daniel stabbed a key. The screen wiped to: 'UK gilt down one point on back of employment figures'.

Daniel mouthed silently but emphatically: *Fuck.*

'I can fill it at ninety-six,' Lennox said.

'I'll break the point with you,' Daniel said quickly.

'Ninety-six,' Lennox insisted.

'No.'

Daniel shut his eyes. In less than five minutes he had clocked up a one million pound loss. He couldn't believe he had made such an arsehole miscalculation. 'Lennox,' he said after a pause, 'I'll talk to you.' He cut the line.

'We're a whole point out of court,' said Jamie.

'I know that!' Daniel snapped. 'Damn it!' He smashed the telephone back onto its cradle. 'This market *has* to turn. . .'

Jamie was staring at him. 'Not our way it won't.'

'*Damn this market!*' Shaking his head in disbelief, Daniel stood. 'This *bloody* market. I'm not doing Lennox any more favours. Tell him, Jamie!'

Jamie looked away. He had seen Daniel blow his stack before; he had seen it happen to everyone in the room, with the possible exception of Robbie Barrell. It was an accepted method of easing pressure.

As Daniel continued to rage, a frisbee drifted behind him and was snatched out of the air by Elana Cimino. Chuckling, she sent it spinning on over Wolfgang Bauer's head.

'I just don't *believe* it,' Daniel hissed.

Two desks away Anna Schumann glanced at him askance, then caught Robbie Barrell's observant eye.

'Danny boy – ' The senior dealer leaned forward over the top of his desk. 'Go home, will you?'

Sighing, seething, grateful, Daniel snatched up his jacket and stalked out.

He drifted all afternoon, from restaurant to pub to wine bar, finding no reason to go home, ricocheting from caustic self-loathing at his own stupidity to a rankling resentment of Anna Schumann, not at all leavened by a degree of pure lust.

And behind it all, smarting afresh every time he tried to argue it away, lay the raw pain of Bonnie.

He didn't want to be in love; he didn't want to feel this exposed, this bloodily vulnerable; he just wanted things the way they had been. Riding the market, enjoying the game, reaping the rewards that came. Onward and upward, not easy but attainable . . . Suddenly it had all got so fucking *serious*; the market, his private life . . .

With a chill of fear he wondered if Tony Eisner had found himself treading a similar path. When you were on top this game was pure electricity sparking through your veins; but on the way down the same high charge could fry you, roast your brains. He had watched it happen enough times before.

He was walking through St Katharine's Dock when he

saw the pay-phone. Without allowing himself to think, he dropped in a coin and dialled Bonnie's number.

'This is Bonnie Deverill. I'm not here at the moment, but leave me a message and I'll get back to you as soon as I can . . .'

Sweet pain uncurled in the bottom of his heart.

He waited until the tape had run, then put down the receiver. And self-loathing returned in a rush of anger. What was the point of kicking yourself in the crutch? You didn't beat the market by brooding, by poring over past blunders; you acted, you moved on. He found another coin and forced himself to dial quickly.

A woman's voice answered.

'Lucy? Lucy – it's Daniel. What are you doing?'

The distant voice was bright, breathless, excited; he felt his spirits lifting already. 'Would you like to have dinner? Yeah, tonight. Seven? Any place you want.' He laughed. 'Yes, I know it. I'll see you – '

He put the phone down again, the first warmth of the day unfolding inside him. Onward, upward; if you gave in you were dead. Then he realized he had an hour to find a clean shirt and a razor blade.

Six

He had forgotten, Daniel decided halfway down their fourth bottle of saké, how devastatingly attractive Lucy was. Quite the opposite type to Bonnie, of course. Long and lean and leggy, a sweeping mane of fine, shoulder-length, light blonde hair, huge eyes, high cheek bones and the kind of pale honey tan it was easy to maintain on BA long haul.

Fortnight-long absences on the far side of the world had made it easy to keep things casual, an arrangement that appeared to suit her as much as him, and the advent of Bonnie had been relatively painless. But he had always kept in touch.

'Listen,' Daniel hiccupped, then giggled as Lucy's neat, pink tongue circled his ear, 'you must, you *must* know someone who wants a hundred million treasury notes.'

Lucy chuckled, her arm looped around Daniel's neck. 'Well . . .' Her forehead puckered thoughtfully. 'What can you use them for?'

Daniel gave an exaggerated shrug. 'You can paper the walls with them. I don't know what else.' He picked up his glass and drained it. 'I'm trying not to think about it.' He reached for his Marlborough packet, a manoeuvre that became easier in the small restaurant cubicle when Lucy unlooped her arm.

'Daniel,' she said more seriously as he lit a cigarette. 'what's up with Bonnie?'

He inhaled quickly. 'It's all finished with Bonnie. She's bored with me. That's the bottom line. And she's found someone else.' He shrugged again, dismissively. 'What can I tell you?'

Gloom radiated suddenly from him with a force that even drunkenness couldn't hide from Lucy. She had just finished a brief but intense liaison in Hong Kong and was in urgent need of a boost to her own spirits. Admitting the faintest hint of depression could ruin both their evenings.

She leaned closer, grinning into his eyes. 'Would you like to eat, Daniel . . .'

Daniel looked up and saw her grin become sly. 'Yeah.' His face lifted at the unspoken invitation. 'I'll get the bill.' He waved at a passing waiter without effect. Shaking his head, he got to his feet, fumbled in his pocket and tossed a fifty pound note down onto the table. Then he guided a smiling Lucy to the door.

He could not fault her.

Her body was supple and slim, her breasts small and round and firm; she responded easily and passionately, drawing him into her as urgently as he felt the need to penetrate, climaxing with a soft, shuddering moan. Physically the sex was very good.

And yet, as he nestled against her rib cage, he felt a fraud. He had put on an act; one that had convinced his own body as well, apparently, as Lucy's. But all the time he had been reaching for more – more intimacy, more contact – and found only gestures, or confusion in familiar places. It was a measure of how much he had taken for granted with Bonnie, how much they had achieved; the last memory he wanted to stir. Now he felt empty and lonely, and slightly foolish. He liked Lucy. He hoped she hadn't noticed.

He blinked awake, hardly conscious that he had slept until his eyes settled on the digital clock next to the bed.

Four thirty.

'Damn!'

He darted a glance at the slumbering form beside him, but there was no movement. Gingerly he slipped out of bed and padded about the carpet in the light from the hall, gathering scattered clothes. His naked foot struck an empty vodka bottle, knocking it into a second. Wincing, he set both upright, and, on impulse, picked up the two overflowing ashtrays next to them and put them on a side table.

He dressed quickly in the hall, tip-toeing the short distance to the front door and sliding out of the flat.

In bed Lucy lay with eyes open, listening to the stealthy sounds of departure, the final, thunderous click of the Yale. *Ah well; you win some, you lose some.* She turned, tucking the duvet around her, and deliberately quashed the stab of regret under a wave of sleep.

Jamie Dunbar glanced at the trading floor clock and swallowed a sigh. Nine thirty, and Daniel's desk conspicuously empty. That was two research calls missed in a row. It was bad enough having to keep covering for Daniel, but after yesterday's cock-up Jamie had enough on his plate. All the markets seemed to be taking a breather: gilts were at a dead stop – not even small buying, let alone the bucketload he had to unload.

'How's it going?'

He looked up at Anna Schumann. Her dress was light blue today – always a strong, plain colour. She looked as immaculate as ever, something Jamie found slightly intimidating. The unspoken rivalry between her and Daniel made his position awkward. But he couldn't help the expression on his face.

'Cleaning up after yesterday's crap shoot?' she asked.

He almost responded to her faint smile, but the professional slur struck home. 'We'll square it off today,' he said, turning abruptly back to his screen.

Anna cocked an eyebrow and strolled back to her desk. She sat, thoughtfully. Daniel's outburst of the previous day had given her a temporary edge, and provided a useful indicator of his character, but she did not underestimate him for a minute. She had studied his record; she knew his reputation. He had produced bouts of inspired dealing she would never match – or want to. Her skills were rooted in good research, good contacts, quick – not wild – thinking. Relying on gut instinct made you too vulnerable, too likely, when it failed, to end up like Tony Eisner. She did not want Daniel as a rival; she simply wanted him out of her way. And it was only a minor irritation that she found him one of the few physically attractive men on the trading floor.

A figure loped past her, catching her eye.

'Wolfgang – how's it going?'

The German paused and made a see-saw motion with his hands. 'Market's going to pep up. New Euro-sterling issue: Stanner Industries.'

Anna brightened immediately. 'Is it swapped?'

Wolfgang shrugged. 'No idea. Give Jerome a call – in capital markets.'

'Thanks, Wolfgang.'

'My pleasure.'

She grinned as he clicked his heels. Conflict sharpened

her, but she also needed friends. Wolfgang departed under the quizzical gaze of Elana Cimino.

'Jerome?' Anna called on an internal line. 'Anna Schumann. I hear we're bringing Stanner Industries to the market today. What's the size of the deal?'

'Hefty.' The accent was Eton-smooth. 'One hundred million.'

'Is it swapped?' Anna asked. 'Who's doing it?' She nodded at the answer. 'Lowenstein's? I have a guy at Lowenstein's. And maturity?' She nodded again. 'Perfect. Do you mind if we have a crack at the gilt trade? Thanks, Jerome.' She cut the line and fingered the Lowenstein tab. 'Hi, George – it's Anna.' She smiled into the phone. 'Yeah, it was a good move for me. How're you?' She laughed at the reply. 'Listen – I've a little exposure here I'd like to re-structure. A hundred million. Gilts: ninety-threes.' She paused. 'We can provide a block trade to hedge your swap for Stanner Industries. Ninety-six and a quarter. I know it's off market, but we can do the size. C'mon – it'll save you shopping. Want to think it over?' Her brow knitted as she got her answer. 'Lunch? Well, I'll give you a definite maybe. Maybe Thursday? OK, bye.'

She put down the phone and sat back, looking at the hunched figure of Jamie Dunbar. Then she turned to her assistant. 'Patrick, how about some coffee?'

'Sure.' He nodded and got up from his desk. Immediately the desk squawk boxes sprang to life.

'We have a new issue on the market. Sterling one hundred million for Stanner Industries. Ten per cent coupon – five years – issue price par and a half. We've got paper to go at less one and three quarters. Make those calls!'

There was an instant flurry of activity from the sales desks fringing the room.

'Roberto,' came the announcement. 'Five million into Italy.'

The Lowenstein tab lighted on Anna's screen. She picked up her phone. 'Anna Schumann.'

'George,' the caller announced himself. 'Yes. We want to trade.'

'Great!' Anna's face lit up. She rose to her feet, turning towards the Far East desk. 'Why don't you call Jamie Dunbar? It's really his position.'

Jamie caught his name and glanced up, his expression wary.

Anna grinned. 'And – hey, George? Lunch is confirmed, Thursday. On me.' Laughing, she replaced the phone.

A tab glowed on Jamie's screen. 'Whitney Paine,' he spoke into the phone and paused. 'Yes, speaking.' His face suddenly registered surprise. 'You do?' He paused. 'One hundred million quote eleven threes – Feb ninety-threes. Price is one oh one.' He waited again. 'Right! You're done.'

He replaced the receiver, a look of incredulous relief spreading across his face. The whole damn lot in one go, plus hefty profit, plus commission. So there *was* a Santa Claus after all! Then his bright gaze crossed Anna's; she was watching him, her smile faint but self-congratulatory. The penny dropped.

Shit.

His growing smile faded abruptly. This was all Daniel needed.

He arrived at noon, looking refreshed, whistling tunelessly, his jacket over his shoulder. He threw a swift, placatory grin in Robbie Barrell's direction.

'Where the hell have you been?' Jamie hissed.

Daniel grimaced and waved a dismissive hand. Sinking into his chair, he punched for the gilt position on his terminal. 'Hey!' he cried suddenly. 'Good work!'

'Not my work,' Jamie said glumly, and tossed his head towards the dollar desk. 'Blondie over there . . .'

Daniel glanced across; she was busy on two phones, talking animatedly. His face darkened. This was not one he should have lost. He threw an annoyed look at Jamie.

The American spread his arms innocently. 'I don't know how – Lowenstein's called. Took the lot. That's all I know.'

Daniel breathed in. She had only been on this floor a couple of days and every public move he'd made had proved he'd have trouble wiping his bottom unaided, let alone running the dollar desk. All this distant manoeuvring was getting him nowhere. He had hardly exchanged half a dozen words with the woman. It was time to move in close.

He got up.

'Where are you going now?' Jamie frowned.

'Trust me,' Daniel murmured, and made for the door.

Ten minutes later he re-appeared, a cone of soft ice cream in each hand. He walked to Anna's desk and planted a haunch on the edge. As she glanced up he presented her with a cone. She looked surprised, but took it.

'I didn't know you played the swaps market,' Daniel said.

'I don't,' she said. 'I've picked it up this morning. It wasn't that difficult.' Her manner was cool; the implication that *some* people succeeded in what they set out to do.

'No,' Daniel agreed. 'I appreciate it. Jamie and I appreciate it.'

'It was your fuck up,' she said flatly. 'Not Jamie's.'

'Jesus!' Daniel glanced across the room and back again. 'What's bugging you?'

She blinked slowly. 'Nothing. Thanks for the ice cream.'

Well, why not just shove it up my nostril? It's obviously what you want to do.

Daniel swallowed mounting anger. He took a deep breath. 'Look – maybe we could have dinner.'

She turned back towards her terminal. 'I'm busy.'

'Tomorrow night?'

She shook her head. 'I'm busy tomorrow night as well.'

'Friday?'

'Friday I'm going home.'

Daniel reached across her desk to the calendar pinned next to the VDU. He leafed brusquely through the pages. 'How about September the twenty-second?' he said. 'That looks blank.'

She turned cold blue eyes on him. 'I never plan that far ahead.'

'OK.' He got up and walked away.

'I'm being straight with you,' she called after him. 'I'm busy.'

Ignoring her, Daniel plumped into his chair, raked the contents of a drawer for a new packet of cigarettes and ripped away the cellophane, buckling the cardboard.

Ice queen. Christ, that wasn't the half of it.

'OK.' He glanced fiercely at an attentive Jamie. 'Let's make money!'

Rachmaninov's second piano concerto thundered from the quad speakers. After *Brief Encounter* it had been one of Bonnie's favourites. Slumped on his living room couch, Daniel thumbed through 'Market-Eye' pages on the Sony remote. His wolfhound, crouched on the floor beside him with its head in his lap, glanced up at the TV screen and yawned spectacularly.

'Listen,' Daniel chided the animal, 'I sit through *Lassie*, don't I? Five more minutes, OK?'

The telephone trilled. He dropped the remote, and rummaged under a jumble of cushions for the cordless. 'Yeah?' His interest flagged instantly as a male voice spoke, and then picked up again just as quickly. 'OK,' he said, suddenly brisk. 'I need an hour. Let's say nine.'

The cocktail bar was shadow-filled, uplit by bright blue neon strips, crowded and raucous. A long window produced dark reflections over views of Thames wharfs.

Sitting at the bar, Daniel glanced at his wristwatch and frowned. Nine ten. He had planned on an early night.

Then a lean, lank-haired young man in bomber jacket and jeans was suddenly at his side. 'Hi,' he said, sniffing.

Daniel gestured to the barman.

'Beer'll be fine,' said the newcomer.

'What have you got?' Daniel asked.

The young man unzipped his jacket, pulled out a large, stiff-backed envelope and slid it along the bar top. Daniel tore it open and took out several typed, stapled sheets and half a dozen eight by ten black and white prints. He began to flick through the sheets.

The young man accepted his beer and sipped. 'She leads a pretty busy social life. But there's just one regular guy.'

Daniel turned to the first print. It showed Anna Schumann beneath the canopied entrance to an apartment block. It was night; one edge of the picture was obscured by what might have been the side of a car window. She was embracing a tall, grey-haired man in a suit, his back to the camera.

Interest quickening, Daniel flicked to the second print. Same point of view. Anna and her friend had turned towards the street; both were laughing. The man was Frank Mallory.

'Those were taken outside her flat,' said the young man, bending closer to look.

'When?' Daniel snapped.

The young man reached across and turned the print over. There was a date printed on the back. 'Three days ago,' he said, sniffing.

The third print showed the couple parting, hands still linked; Mallory wore a Cheshire cat grin.

No wonder the ice queen didn't want to know.

Things were starting to make sense. This was the edge he had been looking for. Smiling faintly, Daniel slipped prints and sheets back into the envelope.

'You want me to carry on?' the young man asked.

Daniel shook his head. 'No. I don't need to know any more.' He touched the other's half-empty glass. 'Have another.'

'No thanks.' Another sniff. The relentless trendiness of the place seemed to unsettle him.

Daniel pulled a smaller, fatter envelope out of his jacket pocket and handed it over. 'Well, thanks – '

The young man glanced into the envelope, and his eyes widened. It was stuffed with twenty pound notes. 'Thank *you*,' he said.

'Right.' Daniel smiled briefly and turned back to his cocktail. The young man nodded and slipped away.

Tony Eisner had used the agency for discreet check ups on dodgy private clients. Daniel was glad he had kept their card, even gladder he had got them working the day Anna Schumann had arrived.

Anna and Frank Mallory. He would be interested to know what Melvin Peters thought of that.

He finished his cocktail and made for the exit, his step light. It was about time the tide turned in his direction.

Seven

'So let's hit it, OK?'

Heads bowed to desks as Robbie Barrell concluded the Monday research call.

Sinking into his chair, Robbie stifled a yawn. He and his wife had had what he called a 'sparky' weekend; verbal pyrotechnics and a lot of aggravation he could happily do without; it was happening more and more these days. On top of that he had been half an hour late: staff shortages on the Fenchurch Street line. He hadn't even stepped into his office yet.

He might try a swift snort in a couple of minutes; it looked like he was going to need it today.

Picking up his document case, he walked over to the trading floor entrance to his office. The glass door rattled under his grasp, and stayed where it was. Jammed? Frowning, he tried again, just as the door to the main hall opened and a grey-shirted security guard came in.

Who the hell had locked his door?

He rattled it again, and became aware of the guard looming at his shoulder.

'You come to fix this thing?' he snapped.

'No, sir.'

Robbie stared at the man; he was heavy and black, his expression wary. 'You what?'

The guard eased in front of him, back to the door, blocking his way.

'What the fuck's going on?' Robbie exploded. 'Why can't I get in here?'

Behind him heads turned; conversations halted. The security guard blinked, abashed but determined. 'I'm sorry, sir. I got my orders from the eighth floor.' He glanced across the room to where three or four dealers, including Daniel, were standing, and his voice dropped fractionally. 'I believe, sir, that you've been dismissed.'

'Dis – fucking – missed!' Robbie roared. He prodded the man's chest. 'How come you know that and I don't?'

The guard blinked again and folded his arms, avoiding Robbie's fierce gaze.

Furious, the senior trader swivelled and headed for the end of the octagon, passing a curious Daniel on the way.

'Maybe I haven't been paying attention,' Robbie shouted. 'I thought I bloody worked here!' He snatched up a phone.

'What's up for Christ's sake?' Daniel asked.

'Where's Frank Mallory?' Robbie cried, face working. With his free hand he pulled a cigar from his jacket pocket, bit off the end, spat it out and applied a cigarette lighter. 'Frank?' he said suddenly. 'Frank – what the hell's going on? My office is locked and there's a guy standing out the front telling me I'm fired. It's not April the fucking first, is it?'

Frowning, Daniel watched Robbie's face as he listened, inhaling deeply. After a pause the older man caught Daniel's eye and shook his head.

'Whose decision and when?' Robbie snapped. He began to nod. 'Frank,' he interrupted, 'don't screw around with me. You want me to carry the can for Tony Eisner, right? Then just fucking say so! I don't want to hear all this crap about our trading profile and third quarter figures – '

He sighed as Mallory continued, then he covered the

mouthpiece and told Daniel: 'I've got the bloody chop!' Immediately he resumed the conversation. 'Well, that's very generous of you, and of the board, Frank. It certainly makes up for the lies and deceit and the treachery. Every time I spend some of it I'll think of you.' He slammed the phone back onto its cradle.

'What the hell is going on?' said Daniel.

Robbie pulled on his cigar and looked at him. 'They needed a scapegoat,' he said stiffly. 'I got the part.' Before Daniel could reply, he turned and strode back to the waiting guard. 'You're going to get a call from upstairs,' Robbie told him. In the meantime I'm going in there to pick up my personal effects.'

The guard glanced at him and away again. 'I haven't received that call yet, sir.'

Robbie nodded darkly. 'Oh. I see. Well, let's put it another way – ' He stepped back, lifted a VDU from the end of the octagon, jerked its cable free, turned and hurled it at the office door. As the guard jumped back, it struck the glass explosively. A hail of splinters burst into the room, leaving an empty frame.

As Robbie moved forward, the guard sprang in front of him. Daniel pushed between them, and the door to the main hall burst open.

'Hey! Hey! Wait!' a girl called. Everyone turned. The petite blonde was Mallory's secretary. 'Mr Barrell is allowed to remove his personal effects,' she told the guard breathlessly. 'You can – ' She caught sight of the hole where the door had been and her voice faltered. 'Let him in.'

'Very well.' The guard gave Robbie a sharp look.

'But I have to be present, I'm afraid, Mr Barrell.' The secretary recovered quickly.

'What?' Robbie tossed over his shoulder. He walked into

his office, kicking aside pieces of splintered wood. 'In case I run off with the paper clips?'

Daniel followed the girl inside.

'You may only remove your personal effects,' she said, and blushed. 'I'm sorry . . . Mr Mallory couldn't . . .'

Pulling open desk drawers, Robbie gave her a look of swift sympathy. 'I know . . . I know . . . Mallory sent you down here. He can't come himself.' He grunted, and plucked a cardboard box from a cabinet. Plumping it on the desk, he began to drop in diaries, family photographs, framed certificates from the wall. The bout of vandalism seemed to have assuaged his anger.

He glanced up at Daniel, even smiled grimly. 'Well, Danny boy, the writing's on the wall. They're going to mount a clean-up operation. They didn't put Anna Schumann in here just because she's a pretty face. They're looking for a safe, orthodox team. You can bet on it.'

Daniel nodded. 'I'm getting the picture.'

In just under a minute the box was full. Ostentatiously the guard unlocked the door to the main hall and held it open. He followed at a discreet distance as Daniel walked Robbie to the lift.

'You'd better watch your arse, Daniel,' Robbie told him.

'Can't we take this to Peters? Higher?'

Robbie shook his head. 'Forget it. It's a good corporate American firing. Nice handshake. Three hundred grand.' He sighed and looked suddenly very tired. 'Look, I'm not complaining. Across the street I'd get fifty quid and a nice cup of tea.'

Daniel smiled faintly as the lift doors opened in front of them.

Cardboard box in his arms, document case under his elbow, Robbie stepped forward into the lift. 'Question is,

Daniel,' he said, turning, 'who's going to be sitting in my chair?'

He winked as the doors thumped shut on him; Robbie Barrell, and eleven years of top class dealing experience, were gone.

He owed Robbie more than he could ever quantify.

Before Whitney Paine he had been brash and lucky; after, he had been brash and skilful; and all the best tricks had come from Robbie. Robbie had taught him how to survive among the big boys – and the big bonuses. Six years of those top earnings had bought him a spread in Kent, a plane, a Facel Vega, a lifestyle he had only dreamed about ten years ago.

And in five short minutes the man who had put all that within his reach had ceased to exist; it was like witnessing a bloody road accident.

Daniel stirred the ice in his empty whisky glass, his back to the sunset view of the Thames which had drawn most of the early evening clientele to the bar.

His second drink and Jamie Dunbar arrived simultaneously.

'Pina Colada,' the young American ordered, slotting into the seat across the table. He screwed up his eyes in the sunset glare. 'How did you get on?'

Daniel shrugged. 'We wait, we see. New client. You never know . . .'

Jamie grunted. Both knew that Daniel's over-extended lunchtime meeting had been an excuse to get out of the office. He had stuck it out until one, hoping against hope for a call from Mallory, knowing in his heart that he stood about as much chance of getting Robbie's job as persuading Bonnie to come back. But that didn't stop the bitterness.

Jamie's cocktail appeared. Daniel waited while he took a deep draught. 'Well?' he said finally. 'Who is it?'

Jamie stretched his lips in a gentle wince. 'Guess.'

'Is there an "A" and an "S" in the name?'

Jamie nodded slowly. 'Yup.'

'First name Anna? Last name Schumann?'

Jamie raised a finger. 'Bingo,' he said.

Daniel gave a hissing sigh and shook his head. Why had he tortured himself by even dreaming it would be different? He drained his glass in one and signalled to the waiter. Then he leaned forward across the table. 'Mallory,' he told Jamie, 'is going to take over the bank. He's got his girlfriend in the hot seat.'

Jamie stared at him. 'Girlfriend? What do you mean?'

Daniel pointed a finger at his assistant's head. '*That* goes firmly under your hat.'

Two more drinks appeared.

Daniel sighed again, more heavily, feeling the alcoholic warmth radiate from his stomach. He hadn't really sobered up from lunchtime. 'Maybe,' he said, 'I should just get out now. There are other banks.'

'Yeah . . .' Jamie spoke warily. He had dealt with a drunken Daniel before; it was either wild euphoria or blank depression, neither of much lasting significance.

Daniel stared at the table top. 'They're going to crucify me.' He hiccupped. 'I wonder where Barrell's going to go? I might join him.' He looked up suddenly. 'What would you do, Jamie?'

'Wait it out. Be patient. Schumann is just the flavour of the month. Give it a while – six months – she'll be history.'

Daniel grunted. He had a lot of respect for Jamie. The American lacked fire, but he had a steadiness Daniel lacked even more.

'I don't think I'll last a couple of months,' Daniel said.

Jamie drained his glass and stared him full in the face. 'I think you should try,' he said.

Eight

'How'd we get into this crap?'

Anna Schumann's voice lifted angrily above the trading floor's late afternoon hubbub. Daniel raised his eyes from his screen. She was standing at the senior trader's desk, leaning over the shoulder of a seated and cowed Patrick Skill, her assistant.

'I told you – I *warned* you!' she cried. 'The guy is the Prince of Darkness, he isn't a registered charity. He wants to *kill* you, OK?'

Daniel hadn't seen her lose her cool before; it was impressive, her looks adding a charge he almost envied Patrick.

The assistant, a stocky, prematurely balding young man, looked sick. 'Alright,' he said awkwardly. 'I took a risk – I –'

Anna's humourless laugh cut him short. 'That wasn't a risk, Patrick. That was suicide!' She reached across him and stabbed keys on his terminal. Both looked at the screen. 'And now we're dead, right?'

Patrick's face dropped even further.

Intrigued, Daniel keyed up the deal on his own screen. Patrick had bought a stack of US Commercial Paper from Salomon's. The US market had been falling steadily for a week, but there had been a pick-up at New York's opening. Only a mild spike, though: all the indicators still pointed downward, which was exactly the way prices had gone moments after Patrick's transaction.

Daniel grunted. They were good salesmen at Salomon's. He picked up his phone and pressed an internal tab.

A light blinked on Anna's screen. She lifted her phone.

Daniel covered a nostril and spoke quickly. 'Call Fred Monroe at Smith New Court. He wanted Yankee paper fifteen minutes ago.'

Across the room he caught the puckering of Anna's smooth forehead. 'Who is this?' As she glanced round the floor, he bowed his head again.

'A friend,' he said. 'Call Fred now. He's packaging something. He could help you.' He put down the phone.

Anna paused, suspicious. She wasn't aware of anyone owing her favours here. In their quaint City way, most had been polite but guarded about her rapid promotion; Robbie Barrell had been well-liked. But she knew Monroe's name. She began dialling.

Watching, Daniel smiled faintly. At his back he heard Elana jousting on the phone.

'Because, Nils,' she cried, 'I don't *want* to spend the weekend in Johannesburg with you. OK? It's nothing personal – it's just that you're a real arsehole. I've never met you and you keep asking me to spend weekends with you!' Her phone crashed back onto its cradle. 'Better to be direct, eh, Wolfgum?'

There was a Teutonic grunt.

On the far side of the octagon Anna's frown was fading fast. 'OK, I'm sorry,' she told her assistant, putting down her phone. 'But next time, watch it.'

Patrick nodded, relieved but still uneasy. The lady clearly didn't like backtracking.

Daniel lifted his phone and punched her number. 'Fred able to help you out?' he asked.

Now the frown was back: she didn't like sharing the glory, either. Her brilliant gaze swept round the room, and faltered as it connected with Daniel.

'Just being neighbourly,' he said, cocked his head and winked.

Two minutes later his own phone flashed.

'Is that dinner invite still open?' she asked.

Daniel paused. 'I got a window about two months from now – '

'Eight o'clock at Mosimann's,' she said tartly. 'My treat.' And cut the line.

Daniel looked up and caught Jamie Dunbar's curious glance. Daniel raised his eyebrows, innocently.

The best deals, Robbie Barrell had once told him, started with the edge. Find the other guy's weak spot – any weak spot; don't overdo it, but always get him on the defensive.

Then do business.

He wondered if Robbie and Anna Schumann had been to the same school.

She had changed into something lighter in colour and shorter-sleeved; not exactly sexy, but it did show him her forearms. He hadn't seen those before. They were unusually attractive forearms. It was deliberate, of course, as was the choice of restaurant table: small, secluded, illuminated by a single candle; the service hushed, discreet, impeccable.

By normal standards – a superb meal finished, the second bottle just opened – he would have thought he was doing well. It disturbed and annoyed him that he still hadn't the faintest idea.

As he lit the third cigarette in ten minutes, she said archly: 'Am I making you nervous or do you always smoke like this?'

'Yup,' he said, and inhaled.

She blinked slowly. 'Which?'

'Always smoke like this.'

She gazed at him steadily for a moment. He looked back, quite impassive, allowing the smoke to curl up from his nostrils. Why did he get the overwhelming impression of a Mexican stand-off?

He raised an eyebrow. 'Do you generally make other people nervous?'

The question seemed to amuse her slightly. 'Not deliberately,' she said.

'Ah.' Daniel nodded. 'It just seems that people around you, on the whole, are unnaturally jumpy.'

Another slow blink. 'I like people to think about what they're doing.'

Daniel smiled. 'They weren't thinking too clearly this afternoon.'

He saw, rather than heard, her intake of breath. Her eyes dropped to neat, beautifully manicured hands.

'I appreciate what you did.'

'I know.' The blandness of Daniel's smile was intended to infuriate. 'We wouldn't be sitting here otherwise.'

She looked at him from under still lowered lashes. 'I wanted . . . well, you know I'm grateful to you.'

'That's OK.' Daniel stubbed out his cigarette vigorously. 'I don't like to see anyone too deep in the shit.'

That stung. Her eyes flared. 'I inherited a situation. You know that. Otherwise I'm running an even book. In any event, *anyone* can make a mistake.' She meant Daniel. 'Or are you the only one in the department who's allowed to screw up?'

He shrugged easily. 'I might take a dive now and again. I always bring it back. Every quarter I'm never less than even. Last returns showed I made three million for the books in a nine-week stretch. Take a look.'

'I did take a look,' she said. 'I read every major deal you've made over the past twenty-four months, and I know you're dangerous.'

Daniel grinned. 'Dangerous?' How nice to be called dangerous by a woman who looked like this.

Her eyes narrowed as she took his meaning. 'Reckless might be a better word.' She paused as Daniel lit another cigarette. 'I don't want anyone under me taking those kind of risks. All right?'

When did Mallory give you that script? Daniel thought. *In bed last night?*

'Is that why you brought me here?' he asked, re-pocketing his lighter. 'To give me a formal warning?'

She gazed at him levelly. 'I don't want to argue with you. And, no, I didn't bring you here to give you a warning.'

Daniel gazed back and felt his stomach sink involuntarily. What did she mean by *that*? The thought of what she would be like in bed – how quickly would the hard-boiled image evaporate? Or would it? – flickered through his mind for the millionth time. 'How about a nightcap?' he said.

She glanced down. 'It's late and I'm tired.'

'I live nearby. In Kent.'

Her look was quizzical. 'That's hardly nearby.'

Daniel raised a finger. 'Twenty minutes – I promise.'

The Cessna landed by the fading glow of sunset, dislodging a flight of Grey Lag geese who departed westward in a flurry of pumping wings. Bringing the aircraft round in a smooth loop, Daniel cut the engine and coasted in to the small landing stage. Anna unclipped her seat belt and regarded him with an amused half-smile: *I am impressed, but don't think that counts for anything.*

Daniel opened the cabin door and hopped out to secure the machine. His wolfhound came loping down the unkempt pathway from the house to greet him.

While Daniel rattled glasses in the kitchen, Anna draped her jacket over the back of an armchair and went on a tour of the Pascoe living room.

It had more character than she had expected – masculine, of course, a lot of browns and creams in natural fabrics, some interesting wall paintings that looked original. Obviously *not* interior designed; she had been prepared for something glitzy and expensive and basically empty. He plainly lived, rather than merely crashed here.

Perhaps he was something more than a market buccaneer. It was this sort of information, she told herself, that had made her accept his invitation.

Her gaze drifted to a group of photographs on a table by the window. Sentiment, even: Daniel posing in Biggles costume next to a battered Tiger Moth; Daniel with a shock-haired man in his sixties, sharing the same brash grin. No sign of females, Anna noted. Her eyes rose to the high, carved pine fireplace, the bric-a-brac of the mantelshelf. Swedish candles, matching pewter mugs . . . she blinked at the eight by ten black and white print positioned in the dead centre.

Her first thought was its total incongruity; her second was that it showed Frank Mallory embracing a fair-haired young woman she recognized, a heart beat later, as herself.

The shock left her bemused, half-disbelieving. She stepped closer.

The picture was taken at night, on the pavement outside her apartment block. There was absolutely no doubt of its authenticity.

Daniel appeared from the kitchen, a glass in each hand, and saw where she was looking. 'Are you interested in photography?' he asked quietly.

She spun, eyes blazing. 'You sonofabitch! You've been having me followed – I don't *believe* this!'

'I was curious,' he said, moving closer and handing her a glass. Her hand, he noted, trembled as she took it. He looked at her over the rim of his own. 'But now I think I understand.'

'Well, I'll tell you something, Pascoe – ' She stabbed her glass at him, heedless of the amber liquid that slopped onto the carpet. 'I was hired for my ability'

'Where?'

'*Damn* you!' For a second he thought she would slap his face, but she reined herself in, visibly. 'I was hired on my merits as a trader. My relationship with Frank Mallory has nothing to do with it.'

Daniel raised an eyebrow. 'Not even a little?'

'None,' she said flatly. 'Whitney Paine came to *me* through a headhunter. At first I turned it down and then they upped the money and I took it. I never even discussed it with Frank.'

Daniel picked up the photograph and pushed it into her hand. Then he flopped onto the couch opposite. He was enjoying himself. 'It's pretty strange,' he reflected, 'that a woman with a week's history in a bank is promoted to head trader over somebody with eleven years' experience, and over me with six. Don't you think?'

'No.' Anna faced him squarely. 'Barrell was running that room as though it was a private party for you and Tony Eisner.' She snorted derisively. 'One hundred *million* dollars! I'm surprised you weren't fired along with him.'

Daniel sipped at his drink. 'I could go to any room in London and get hired like that.' He snapped his fingers.

Anna slapped her glass down on the mantelpiece. 'I'd be surprised if you would find a job shuffling currency in some deadbeat offshore bank.'

'I get offers twice a month,' Daniel smiled.

'Well,' Anna glared, 'Maybe you should think about taking one of them.' She threw down the photograph, crossed the room and snatched her jacket off the armchair. 'I'd like to go home now,' she announced.

Daniel stared into his glass and swirled its contents thoughtfully. 'Hmmm,' he said.

'Will you take me home, please?' Improbably, Anna's tone grew even icier.

Daniel grimaced. 'It's tricky. Getting off the lake at night . . . you can hit a log or something.'

'I'm sure you've done it before.' Anna's eyes flickered round the room, glimpsed the cordless phone. 'Then call a cab. They do have cabs out here, don't they?'

'There *is* a town about four miles away,' Daniel agreed; then frowned. 'I don't know if the guy'll come out here this time of night.'

Anna paused. Daniel sipped again, feeling her unease all the way across the room, and waiting for a hint of panic. Instead she said angrily, 'Goodnight, Pascoe!'

He glanced up to catch her disappearing through the hall door. It slammed behind her; so did the back door.

Daniel smiled, snatched a packet of cigarettes off a coffee table and swung his legs up onto the couch. It made a deeply satisfying change to see the steel-clad Ms Schumann on the defensive. It would be even more interesting in a few minutes: the nearest road was a single track lane. A rutted, hundred yard long driveway led to it. She would be lucky to find *that* in the dark.

He was deciding whether to offer his couch first, or his bed straightaway, when he heard the Cessna's engine burst distantly into life. Frowning, he half rose, just as the engine noise climbed steeply in pitch.

'Shit!'

He flung himself off the couch and across the room. Yanking open the back door, he saw the red, rotating beacon on the seaplane's tail already halfway across the pale oval of the lake. The aircraft was turning into the wind. As he stared in disbelieving horror, it picked up speed, came unstuck and lifted smoothly over a distant silhouette of trees. He watched the tiny, winking star of the tail light execute an elegant turn and fade in the direction of London.

Then he resumed swearing.

Nine

The mini-cab lost its way en route to the house; it deposited Daniel at Tonbridge British Rail station in time for a train cancellation. He travelled, haltingly, to London Bridge in a carriage too packed to open his copy of the FT.

By the time he reached the bank, just after nine, he was steaming, figuratively and literally. One look at his face persuaded Jamie Dunbar to keep things simple. 'Max called from Salomon's,' he said. 'He doesn't want to deal.'

'No big surprise.' Daniel thumped his document case onto the floor, shrugged off his jacket.

'Jimmy Slaughter cancelled lunch.'

'Thank Christ.' Daniel plumped into his chair, began leafing hurriedly through written messages.

'Your car's fixed.'

'Oh?' he brightened fractionally. 'About time. How much?'

'Three thousand quid. And some change.'

Daniel whistled. That was a year's appreciation up the spout.

'They had to ship a part from France,' Jamie added.

Daniel glanced at the wall clock. 'Anything on the research call?'

'Haven't had it yet.'

Daniel looked at Jamie for the first time. The American shrugged. Daniel risked his first glance in the direction of Anna Schumann's desk. It was empty.

The door to the senior trader's office opened and shut. Anna exited at speed, face set in a frown. She swept through the octagon, tossing a key in Daniel's direction; he had to slap his hand onto his desk to stop it crashing into his Reuters screen. 'It's at Tower Bridge, shithead!' she snapped, not looking at him. 'And your altimeter doesn't work.'

Daniel swivelled in his chair. 'I'm getting that fixed –'

'Don't bother. Maybe you'll smack into something and do us all a favour.'

Frowning, he watched her disappear through a side door. What the hell was so important it justified postponing a research call?

Anna knocked lightly on the door of Lee Peters' office and walked straight in. A night of kids' games with the office yahoo had not left her in an equable mood; she resented being dragged off the dealing floor during a vital trading period.

Peters and Frank Mallory rose from either side of the room's large desk, both smiling a little awkwardly. For an instant she assumed they were apologetic because of their timing. Then it struck her that such niceties weren't the prerogative of senior management and she became suspicious.

After greetings, Lee Peters indicated the chair next to Mallory. Exchanging impassive looks with him, she sat. Why hadn't he given her any prior clues if something was up?

'Anna,' said Peters, 'I'm sorry to bring you up here at this time of the morning. You're busy, I know.'

'I have a research call in fifteen minutes,' she said crisply. Peters' attempts at bonhomie impressed her no more than they had Robbie Barrell. But she was surprised when his awkward smile returned.

'Right . . . well, I'll get right to the point. As you know we publish third quarter figures a little over three weeks from now. I've been reviewing the dollar position since you joined us and I – we – ' he nodded toward Mallory, who smiled briefly – 'are pleased; pleased and encouraged to see that the book is running smoothly. Our concern – ' the smile became rueful; he rubbed the side of his nose, not meeting her gaze – 'is the considerable loss that our dollar operation still reflects . . .'

Christ, it's a lynching party.

Adrenalin began to pump through Anna's veins.

'A loss you inherited, of course,' Mallory chimed in. She ignored him.

'Absolutely.' Peters nodded again. 'But one to which we must address ourselves.' His eyes dropped to the only sheet of paper on his desk. 'I see that you've reduced the situation by some two point three million dollars over the past month and a half.'

Anna cut across him. 'We're talking about a one hundred million dollar negative position.'

'Anna – ' Mallory's voice was soft. 'It's a tough situation. We know that. That's why we engaged you. We know you're capable of handling it. We're under pressure as well.'

Her head snapped towards him. 'Are you saying you're not satisfied with my performance, Frank?'

She saw the private innuendo strike home, but Mallory's gaze remained impassive. 'Absolutely not,' he said smoothly. 'But Lee and I have been talking about ways of speeding up this recovery process.'

'That's right,' Peters nodded.

Anna blinked at him and crossed her legs. Her heart was thumping. What game was this? Who was leading this attack?

'One scenario – I guess that's the right word – ' The American smiled again – 'is a possible incorporation of styles.'

Anna frowned. 'An incorporation of styles?'

'Yes. You're aware, of course, that the bank wishes to squash this reckless trading image that the dollar operation developed under Robert Barrell. At the same time,' Peters hesitated and gave the lightest of shrugs, 'we have to acknowledge that Pascoe – well – he does get results.'

Anna felt the colour drain from her cheeks. 'I don't understand.'

Mallory glanced quickly at Peters, then bent his head towards her. 'What Lee is saying, Anna, is that, at least until we have this dollar situation straight, there might be some percentage in utilizing your talents and Pascoe's in some sort of joint operation.'

The utter disbelief was clear in her face. '*What?*'

'A sort of team effort,' Peters chimed in.

Anna stared from him back to Mallory. 'I need someone I can trust,' he had told her. 'Someone I can rely on to clean up a godawful mess. You'll have a totally free hand, complete backing all the way up to the eighth floor. You have my word on that.'

Where is your goddamn word now, Frank?

His grey eyes dropped momentarily to her breasts, and rose again. 'That's right,' he said easily. 'A team effort.'

I see, Frank; I get the picture. You're a shit like all the others, right?

'What happens when we disagree?' she snapped. 'Flip a coin?'

Mallory settled back in his chair. 'It's an idea we've been discussing, Anna. We naturally wanted to discuss it with you.'

Anna nodded. 'Have you discussed it with Pascoe?'

Peters shook his head. 'Absolutely not.'

'Right.' Anna sprang to her feet, eyes flaring. 'Well, I'd be grateful if you'd consider it discussed and declined. A plan like that could backfire and you'd be looking at a three, four hundred million dollar loss. I'm telling you, the guy should be in a straitjacket!'

The two men blinked up at her, startled by the sudden venom. Peters recovered first. 'So you're opposed to this idea?'

'Totally,' Anna said.

There was a pause. Both men exchanged glances, then stood.

'Right, OK, Anna,' said Mallory. 'Your position's noted. But it's an option which we may yet have to consider.'

Anna glanced at her wristwatch. 'Can you excuse me?'

'Right.' Peters was practically effusive. 'Fine – thanks for coming up.'

She turned and left without another word.

Peters and Mallory raised eyebrows at each other. Then Peters sank back into his chair. 'Well!' he said, clicked his teeth and glanced out at the eighth storey view of the City. When he looked back at Mallory he was smiling. 'I think that's going to work out just fine, don't you?'

Ten

Falling heavy and hard, the rain sluiced down Old Broad Street, spurring rush hour stragglers towards Liverpool Street Station. Though it was only just after seven, street-lamps had activated and the roadway had filled with shuffling, blue-lit taxis.

Head shielded beneath a light raincoat, Anna hovered, frowning, at the kerbside outside Whitney Paine. The rain was annoying. She had planned a busy evening packing and an early night. Frank was picking her up at nine in the morning. They were spending the weekend in the Cotswolds. It would be the first chance she had to quiz him on Peters' 'incorporation of styles' speech.

She didn't intend to give him an easy time.

She became aware of someone pausing a few feet away, turned and saw Daniel, also beneath a raincoat and looking in the opposite direction. Her frown deepened. She moved a couple of paces along the kerb.

'Where are you going?' he asked.

'Home.' She didn't turn. A taxi ducked out of the flow on the opposite side of the road and was seized on before its passengers had disembarked. Anna swore under her breath.

'Where's home?'

'Mayfair. Christ!' She turned with a withering look. 'Why are you asking *me*? You must know where I live. You know everything else.'

'I can give you a lift.' Daniel glanced at the traffic. 'You're not going to get a taxi.'

Anna stared resolutely into the downpour. She sighed softly.

Their footsteps rang in the broad, concrete vault. The car stood on its own, gleaming a rich, metallic blue in the skimped neon of the underground park.

Anna shook her umbrella while Daniel opened the front passenger door for her. She climbed inside onto soft, pale blue leather upholstery. Daniel shut the door, skipped around the long, low, broad body and slid into the driving seat. The six-litre engine purred into life. Instrument lighting spread a warm, buttery glow over the polished walnut fascia.

The 1956 Facel Excellence – the twenty-second example of the only one hundred and fifty-two ever built – moved smoothly towards the exit ramp. Anna's pained silence did not discomfort Daniel unduly. It was no worse than the treatment he had had all week. He had decided to split the honours as far as their last evening went. Now he was simply enjoying the chance to drive; he had only collected the car from the garage at lunchtime.

They swept up St James, and slowed as they crossed Piccadilly. Daniel glanced questioningly at his passenger. 'Curzon Street, isn't it?'

'South Audley Street.' She gazed steadily through the windscreen, hands folded over her document case. 'Behind Grosvenor House.'

He nodded and turned towards Berkeley Square.

'I thought you flew everywhere,' she added.

He ignored the note of derision. 'I just had this fixed. It

was in the garage for three months. I hit a truck. Had to have a new radiator shipped from France.'

Her eyes dropped to the car's interior. 'It's very beautiful,' she said.

'Thank you.' It pleased him that her scorn at least didn't extend to his possessions.

Reaching forward, she lifted an unlabelled cassette from a rack beneath the glove compartment.

'Paderewski,' he said.

She pushed the cassette into the dashboard player. Soft piano music filled the car. Daniel caught her eyebrow lift: appreciation? Surprise? Either was a step up from scorn.

The music carried them into South Audley Street, where the car phone warbled. Daniel ignored it. Anna glanced at him, then, when the warbling showed no sign of abating, picked up the receiver. It didn't surprise her to hear a female voice.

'Just a moment,' Anna said. 'I'll see if he's in.' She pushed the receiver towards Daniel, covering the mouthpiece. 'A young lady – called Lucy.'

Daniel looked pained. He took the phone. 'Hello, Lucy – yeah, I got your message.' He paused. 'Oh that was Anna. She's just someone I work with.'

A wry smile played about Anna's lips.

'Lucy,' Daniel went on, 'can I call you in an hour or so?' He paused again. 'Well, I don't know. Maybe I can make dinner.' He nodded. 'Yeah, I'll call you. Right.'

Anna watched him as he replaced the phone. He stared out at the rain-lashed buildings. 'Whereabouts?'

Anna pointed to a maroon and gold awning on the left. He glided to a halt beside it. A uniformed doorman appeared from a brightly lit interior and opened Anna's door.

'I don't suppose,' Daniel said, turning towards her, 'I could come up for a drink on this damp evening?'

Anna smiled sweetly. 'No, you're right. I don't suppose you could. But thanks for the ride.' She stepped out of the car.

Daniel stretched quickly across the passenger seat. 'Lunch tomorrow?'

Her smile sharpened. 'I'm away for the weekend.'

The doorman snapped the door shut. Daniel's expression was sour. If he hadn't known better, he'd have suspected the woman was beginning to enjoy this.

The rain eased as he turned into Park Lane. He debated whether or not to call Lucy back. A week's duelling with the ice queen had left him drained. He badly needed recreation, but something more than the purely physical kind. He stamped ruthlessly on thoughts of Bonnie.

Re-entering Piccadilly, he was immediately caught in a snarl-up which reduced him to walking pace. Restless, he scanned the passing crowds. He found himself staring at a familiar figure about to enter the doors of the Park Lane Hotel. Instantly he thumped on the horn. The figure turned, frowned, then his face lightened. He strode across the pavement to the car, as Daniel wound down the passenger window.

'Hello, Daniel! How are you, love?' Grinning broadly, Robbie Barrell thrust his head into the car. 'Long time – missed you.'

'Where are you going?' Daniel asked.

Robbie nodded back towards the hotel. 'In here. The Park Lane. Come and have a drink.'

Grinning, Daniel pulled onto the double yellow lines. He had forgotten the fun he'd had under Robbie's regime. Suddenly all that semed an age ago, but his spirits were lifting for the first time in days. 'Are you meeting someone?' he asked as they crossed the hotel's entrance lobby.

Robbie shook his head. 'No; I'm living here.' He winked at the slim, blonde desk clerk, who smiled and fetched his key. They moved towards the lifts. 'Sheila and me – we packed it in.'

'Shit,' Danie frowned. 'I'm sorry, Robbie.'

The older man shrugged. 'That's OK. It was on the rocks anyway. Then this big wave came!' He laughed, a little too carelessly, as the lift doors opened. 'It washed me away.'

They stepped inside. 'So what did you do?' Daniel asked. 'Are you working?'

'No, not working, Daniel.' Robbie was vague. 'Been looking around, but I can't find anything I like. Not sure about the financial world anymore.' He gave Daniel an ironic glance. 'I won't ask you about your life. I suppose it's littered with broken hearts.'

Daniel grunted. 'Just my own.'

The lift doors opened on a long, richly carpeted corridor. Two small Oriental girls, dressed in dark pink stewardess uniform, were approaching.

'Riki!' Robbie cried, bounding forward. He clapped an arm round the prettiest, who giggled brightly. Daniel swapped a bemused smile with her companion.

'Just in from Singapore?' Robbie asked.

'That's right, Bobby,' the pretty one smiled. 'And we got stacked up over Rome for an hour.'

Robbie pulled a face. 'When do you turn around?'

'Two days.'

'We must have dinner.'

The girl twisted in his grasp, almond eyes flashing. 'No

more sushi,' she declared, and turned to Daniel. 'Last time he had to stick his fingers down my throat.'

Robbie spread his arms. 'What are friends for!'

The girls departed in a shower of giggles.

'I love that girl, Daniel,' Robbie said.

Daniel looked at him. 'Really?'

'Yeah,' Robbie nodded. 'It's either that or she won't sleep with me. I can't figure out which.'

Daniel chuckled.

Robbie unlocked his door, flicked on the lights and ushered Daniel into the sitting room beyond. 'Drink, Daniel?' he boomed, striding to a small cabinet. 'Scotch, right?'

Daniel nodded, and moved towards an armchair. The room was large, comfortable and quite impersonal, Robbie's presence marked only by a scattering of newspapers and paperbacks, a framed photograph of his wife, and, Daniel noted on a side table, his trading certificate.

Robbie plumped a glass half-full of neat whisky on the coffee table in front of Daniel. Then he fetched another glass and the bottle and slumped onto the sofa opposite.

'So. Here I am,' he announced, sweeping an arm around. He grinned. 'This is home.'

Daniel didn't smile back. No one in their right mind called a moneypit like this home when they were out of work.

He sipped at his drink. 'Do you see Sheila at all?'

Robbie snorted, leaned forward and tugged a film canister from his jacket. 'You know the old saying? Nobody loves you when you're down and out. Most of the people I know, in the market – ' he made a face and sliced his hand through the air, 'evaporated . . . Fuck them.' He prised open the film canister with his thumb, poked inside with his door key and drew out a generous amount of white powder. Setting the canister down on the coffee table, he snorted quickly. 'Here.' he said, brushing loose grains into his nostrils. 'Try it; it's the nicest stuff I've had in weeks.'

Daniel shook his head. The man was coming apart in front of him.

Robbie reached down and pushed the whisky bottle across the table. 'Never pour a gentleman his drink,' he grinned. 'Isn't that what they say?'

Daniel nodded at the film canister. 'You're into that stuff in a big way, Robbie.'

'That?' Robbie shrugged. 'I can handle that.' He took a deep slug of his Scotch and slumped back again, blowing out his cheeks.

'What's it costing you to live in this place?' Daniel asked.

Robbie raised his eyebrows. 'I don't know. About four grand a week. Plus room service, bar, so on . . .'

Daniel breathed out gently. He had seen this happen to young men, stupid men, men he had always regarded as weak; not to the smart guys like Robbie Barrell.

And Tony Eisner?

The thought brought him up short. He put down his whisky. 'You can't stay here, Robbie,' he said. 'It's like watching yourself go broke.'

Robbie fumbled a packet of cigarettes from his pocket. He lit one from a booklet and tossed away the match. 'I *am* broke, dear boy,' he said, smiling softly.

Eleven

It wasn't often in the past six years that Daniel had had a chance to be generous. He repaid personal debts, yes, but strictly on a quid pro quo basis. Spontaneous favours were a dangerous luxury. At best, a sign of softening. At worst, a slowly ticking time bomb.

But then, he told himself, as he drove Robbie Barrell and four bulging suitcases up the rutted entrance track to his house, he wasn't really being generous. The debt he owed Robbie went deeper than any single deal, or even a whole bundle of them. If anyone had a stake in Daniel's nest egg it was Robbie Barrell.

Daniel flicked on the light of his guest bedroom – in fact, the only other bedroom in the six-bedroom house he had got round to furnishing.

'You can use this room,' he said, stepping aside for the older man.

Robbie squeezed past, dumping suitcases on the pale carpet. Uncurtained windows gave a moonlit view of the lake. He sat on the end of the bed. 'I appreciate this, Daniel. Really I do. I'll get fixed up soon.' He looked old and tired.

Daniel shook his head. 'Stay as long as you want. Sleep well, Robbie.'

He closed the door. Then he went and made his peace with Lucy. Half an hour later he was soaking in a foam-filled bath, sipping Scotch and nibbling on a late night snack of oven chips; they were wrapped in smoked salmon and dunked in mayonnaise. Sibelius' 'En Saga' boomed from a portable CD.

Pausing from the Scotch, he placed his glass on the edge of the bath and reached over to a large brown envelope on an adjacent chair. He opened it and let the glossy, black and white prints inside winnow out onto the foam. Images of Anna Schumann stared up at him: leaving her apartment building, entering, walking along the street. Daniel felt his stomach contract. Even captured at random like this, she looked extraordinarily pretty.

Ball-buster.

He picked a head and shoulders shot and propped it against the whisky bottle, leaving the rest to sink.

The Mallory connection was a useful long stop, but too risky in the short term. He still hadn't got his edge. And he clearly wasn't going to find it in her bed.

Things were going to move soon – they had to; an even book wouldn't recoup the bank's dollar losses in under a year. Lee Peters was going to realize that soon, whatever Frank Mallory said. Daniel had to be ready.

Perhaps more lateral thought was needed.

Pondering, he sank down into the foam. After a long moment he smiled.

He woke at one the next afternoon and found the house empty. In the kitchen was an empty coffee cup, a glass smelling of whisky and several cigar butts. Through the window he caught sight of Robbie wading through the unkempt grass at the lakeside, stick in hand, wolfhound trailing inquisitively. Daniel found it asleep in the kitchen the night before.

Fat lot of use you are as a guard dog, he thought. The pair had obviously made their own introductions.

Robbie was dressed in a shapeless pullover, jeans and wellingtons. He looked as if he had been patrolling these acres since birth. Grinning, Daniel went and got dressed.

At seven o'clock he was in town, stepping out of a taxi beneath the maroon and gold awning in South Audley Street, carrier bag in hand.

The doorman of the previous night opened the main door for him.

'Good evening.' Daniel smiled brightly. 'Miss Schumann in?'

'No, sir. She's away for the weekend.'

'Ah, right.' Daniel nodded as if suddenly remembering. 'May I go up and leave something for her? He raised his carrier bag. 'Just slip it through the letter box. Sort of a surprise.'

The man hesitated. Daniel fingered the twenty pound note in his pocket.

'Yeah, OK,' the doorman drawled suddenly. 'I recognize you – the Italian car, right? Eighth floor. Apartment E.'

Smiling, Daniel made for the lift.

On Anna's floor the corridor led off to the right. Half a dozen doors were visible, Anna's in the middle. No one appeared to be about.

Kneeling, Daniel unzipped his leather jacket and let a cellophane bag of party balloons and a small metal cylinder drop onto the carpet. Then he pulled out a packet of cigarettes and used them to prop open Anna's letter flap. Taking the first of twenty bright blue, sausage-shaped balloons, he hung one end through the door and attached the metal cylinder. He opened the valve at the top and the balloon inflated rapidly to its full eighteen inches. Turning off the valve, he tied a knot in the balloon's end and let it go. It rose rapidly inside Anna's hallway. Glancing around, he started on a second balloon.

He had reached a dozen when a door opened at the end of the corridor. A small, blonde-haired girl of about ten exited carefully, leading a dachshund. She slowed as she approached Daniel, studying him with a bemused smile.

He smiled back, inflated another balloon and held it out to her. 'Here,' he said. 'You haven't seen anything.'

After a pause she took it. He immediately inflated another and handed her that, too.

She laughed, juggling the dog lead to hold both. 'What are you doing? You're mad!'

'Isn't everyone?' said Daniel.

The girl laughed again and moved past him towards the lift.

Daniel removed the cigarette packet from the letter flap and held it open with his fingers as he squinted inside.

In the dimness inside the balloons were just visible, bobbing gently against the hallway ceiling.

Daniel sat back with a satisfied grunt. 'Figure that out,' he murmured.

It was dusk when the Cessna approached the house once more. Daniel was surprised to see two parallel lines of lights where the lake should have been. Confused, he scrabbled for a map, until he realized the lights were *in* the water. A landing path, some thirty feet across, and as many yards long, had been installed down the centre of the lake.

Robbie.

What the devil had he been up to?

Chuckling, Daniel brought the plane down onto the water. Behind him the lights bobbed and weaved in his

wake, making the spray sparkle. Slowing, he peered out of
the cabin window. Each light was a glowing plastic ball,
apparently secured from beneath. At the jetty he found a
thick, black cable climbing out of the water, running along
the boards and disappearing into the grass in the direction
of the house.

Shaking his head, Daniel strode up the path. Lights
shone in the kitchen. As he approached the back door
something shuffled in the semi-darkness of the rear lawn.
Daniel started at the sudden vision of an elderly man,
kneeling on the grass some four or five yards away, staring
at him. As he blinked in shock, the head darted away and
he saw the long, grey body of a goat.

He hiccupped with laughter, then again as a second goat
padded after the first. 'Christ, Robbie; is this a zoo or an
annexe to Gatwick!' he cried, bursting into the kitchen.

Robbie looked up from the table and grinned hugely.
'Hello, sunshine! Hope you're hungry.'

The table was spread from end to end with food: salads,
crêpes, freshly baked rolls, a dazzling array of hors
d'oeuvres. Something crackled and hissed in the oven. The
smell was delicious.

'Bloody hell . . .' Daniel breathed.

'Got the lights off a company I helped float about five
years ago,' Robbie said easily. 'They're only just down the
road. Luck, eh? Saw the goats on the way back. Dead
cheap. They'll have your grass down in a week. Cheers!'
He poured out a glass of wine and handed it to Daniel.
'Drink up!' he laughed.

Daniel drank.

Three hours later, surrounded by the debris of a sensa-
tional duck à l'orange, a remarkable syllabub and two
empty Chablis bottles, they had moved on to Scotch.

'Where'd you learn all this?' Daniel asked.

Robbie drained his glass. 'I'll tell you: before I started mucking around with money I was a cook. Four years at the Savoy, and a couple more in Chicago. I used to be pretty good. I'd forgotten I could do it.'

Daniel grinned. The man was a perpetual surprise. In six years he had hardly scraped the surface.

'You should've invited your friend – what's her name? That stewardess – '

Robbie swallowed and nodded. 'Oh yeah. Riki.'

'Brighten the place up a little.'

Robbie looked doubtful. 'Ah, I've flogged that to death. She says she doesn't want to ruin our friendship. Doesn't want to complicate things.' He shrugged. 'I told her, history is littered with great romantic associations that were born out of friendships.' He reached for his glass. 'Napoleon and Josephine . . . Antony and Cleopatra . . . Hitler and Eva Braun . . .'

'Sonny and Cher,' Daniel offered.

'Right! Right!' Robbie stabbed a finger and burst out laughing.

'You're lending weight to my argument.'

The laughter rumbled to a halt. Daniel burped softly, his senses swimming lazily through alcohol.

Robbie drew in breath, his face growing serious. 'I've seen more marriages than deals fall apart in this racket. No one's got time for anything, except the market . . . It's a bloody circus. I'm glad I'm out.'

Daniel looked at him. 'Are you?'

'Yeah.' Robbie drained his glass. 'Who needs that shit? You've got people burned out at thirty, thirty-five. Nerves in shreds, unemployable. They can't think anything but numbers. It's a power trip – a drug. Where else are you going to get a high like that?'

He answered his own question by fishing his film canister out of his jeans pocket. As Daniel watched, he used the handle of a teaspoon to convey the grains to his nose.

'No less of a drug than this bloody stuff,' he said, and sniffed.

Daniel felt some of his alcoholic glow receding. 'I wish you could ease off the booze or the coke or the cigars.'

Robbie laughed. 'Cold turkey! I'll quit all of them. Nine am.'

'I'm serious,' said Daniel. 'None of this is any good. None of it.'

Robbie's grin faded. 'They're my friends, Daniel,' he said. 'My companions. I can rely on them.'

Clapping his hands round the Scotch bottle, he rose stiffly to his feet. He hiccupped and swayed gently. 'You know, Daniel, the world is not a rotten place. It's just shitheads like us and all the others who've made it this way . . .' The last words slurred, and he dismissed them with a wave of his hand. He started across the room. 'Goodnight, Danny boy – '

Closing his eyes, Daniel heard the door slam. He laid his head carefully down on the table. *A bloody good evening*, he told himself. *Bloody, bloody good evening*.

Then everything went blank.

Anna Schumann unlocked the door to her flat, stepped into her hallway and switched on the light.

'What on earth . . . ?' She hiccupped with laugher.

Coming up close behind her with a suitcase, Frank Mallory followed her gaze up to the ceiling. 'Looks like – a bunch of blue balloons,' he said, bemused.

'Yeah.' Anna grinned 'But how?'

'And who?' Frank frowned.

'No one has a key – ' said Anna, and shook her head.

Chuckling, she moved through into the lounge, only thinking of intruders as she put the light on. But the room was as she had left it. Behind her she heard Frank depositing her suitcase in the bedroom.

The balloons added the final touch to a curious weekend. A weekend full of reassurances, both physical and verbal; perhaps more physical than verbal. Sometimes it seemed that Frank was trying to convince her all was well by force of passion alone. She had decided that wasn't a compliment. Pouring two drinks, she wondered, not for the first time, whether or not she was in love with him. Admiring, desiring, liking; were they the same?

Her relationships had coincided with her career interests before. She liked to think that was more good luck than good judgement.

Frank's arms closed round her waist. As she smiled, he kissed her neck. 'Come and take the weight off your feet,' he murmured.

As soon as they had made love, Frank went and showered, and she knew he would be spending Sunday night at home. She didn't mind – she had reports to read. But, as Frank slipped back from the bathroom, sat beside her on the bed and took her hand, every movement spelled guilt.

'Shu, love,' he said. The pet name was her favourite. 'I've got a week's holiday coming up. We could go to the Mediterranean – '

'Shouldn't you spend it with your children?' she asked.

His earnest expression wavered. 'Ah. I'm taking them to Sardinia in a couple of months.'

'Good.'

He looked awkward. 'I – you know – '

Anna smiled. It still astonished her that a man with Frank's ruthlessness in business could be so inept in emotional matters. 'Frank,' she said, 'you don't have to explain anything to me. I don't mind you talking about your wife, or your children. We've been through all that.' She leaned forward in bed and kissed him. 'Florence would be nice.'

Frank's face brightened. 'Florence it is,' he promised.

She went to sleep alone and dreamed of a continuous stream of balloons filling up her flat from the ceiling down. Frank tried to stop them, but there were so many he was eventually pushed right out of a window.

She also dreamed of Daniel Pascoe.

Twelve

Jamie Dunbar decided that, on the whole, he preferred life to be simple. A deal was good or bad. Daniel was either wildly ebullient, and therefore interesting company, or frenetic and foul, and best avoided. A pensive Daniel, particularly if the mood lasted beyond the second drink of the evening, was simply confusing.

'You're wearing your enigmatic expression,' Jamie prompted.

Daniel stirred the ice in his whisky. 'I sense something cooking,' he said.

'Where?'

Jamie glanced round the crowded cocktail bar. They were sitting at a favourite table, hard up against the picture window with its panorama of the Thames. Three tables away two girls in business suits, one angular, blond and striking, sat together. Jamie saw the blonde glance their way and realized Daniel had caught her eye.

A waiter appeared. Daniel indicated the girl. 'Would you ask the young lady if I might buy her a drink?'

The waiter, who was young and tall, looked doubtful over his dickey, but he nodded and moved away.

'Cooking where?' Jamie persisted.

Daniel leaned back in his seat. 'Upstairs,' he said.

'Excuse me, sir – ' The waiter had re-appeared. Daniel looked up at him.

'The young lady says to piss off.'
Jamie hid his grin in his cocktail glass.

Gone nine, Daniel had had enough. The day had been so-so, his interaction with Anna Schumann minimal. He felt in a hiatus, too vague to get a grip on the market, or his private life. Pushing towards the exit with Jamie, he wondered if he was just horny, when he came face to face with Bonnie.

He blinked in disbelief, ice descending in his stomach.

She looked astonishingly familiar, astonishingly attractive. It threw him even more when her sudden smile was not fey or endearing, but bright and confident.

'What are you doing, Daniel?'

His gaze flickered to her companion. Tall, blond, extremely good-looking. *Christ, she's going out with a beach god.*

'Drinking,' Daniel managed. 'You know. End of the day . . . er, how are you?'

'OK – fine – OK.' She nodded. 'We're meeting some people here.'

Her companion smiled by way of confirmation. He seemed supremely untroubled by Daniel's appearance.

'Ah,' said Daniel, 'we, er – '

'Have to meet some people as well,' Jamie finished brightly.

'That's right,' Daniel chimed in. 'We do.'

Jamie moved round him and held open the door.

'See you around,' Daniel said to Bonnie, as lightly as he was able.

'Bye, Daniel.' She turned away easily and was gone.

So ordinary. So normal.

Standing on the dark pavement, he fumbled for a cigarette. Intellectually he had known they were finished; emotionally, not until this moment. He felt almost physically sick.

Jamie, who had drawn ahead, realized he was alone and turned back, hands in pockets. 'Hey, Daniel.' He winked. 'Great-looking girl!'

The call from the eighth floor came at eight o'clock the next morning, fifteen minutes before a scheduled research call. In the lift Daniel calculated the odds between dismissal and promotion to the dollar desk, and got nowhere.

He was wrong on both counts.

Peters sat behind his desk, Frank Mallory in front of it. Neither rose as Daniel entered.

'We've taken a position about the dollar operation, albeit a temporary one,' Mallory said at once. 'The position is this: you and Anna Schumann are to run the book together until such time as we recover from this negative position. Anna will continue as principal trader and will maintain overall responsibility for the dollar book.'

Daniel frowned. It was a hotch-potch.

'Why not just give me the dollar operation?' he said. 'You want me to be a second player under Schumann?'

Peters' gaze was steady. 'We don't feel secure in giving you the dollar book. Alright? We nonetheless recognize your ability. To put it bluntly, we want the ability without the risk.'

Daniel couldn't suppress a slight smile. 'Anna's not getting results, eh?'

'Anna's getting results,' said Peters coolly. 'We're very pleased with her. We need to get results faster. Alright? That's our position.'

'I don't like it.'

'We've sweetened the deal a little for you,' Frank Mallory added. Daniel looked at him. They had to be getting bloody desperate if Mallory was prepared to be amenable.

Peters leaned forward fractionally. 'This does not leave the room. It's a verbal undertaking made by me in the presence of Frank. Alright?'

Daniel nodded faintly.

'We'll double your commission points on what you do in the next twelve months – if you resolve this dollar loss. You have a virtual free hand. Anna is merely there – how shall I put it? – to avoid major accidents.' Peters consulted an open file on his desktop. 'You could be looking at six hundred grand.' His pale eyes glittered behind his spectacles. Daniel felt his blood quicken, his confidence surge. At last they were starting to talk sense. His smile returned. 'You want me to troubleshoot Anna's book out of the shit?'

Peters' expression was stony. 'In a word,' he said, 'yes.'

'If I pull it off,' said Daniel, 'I want the dollar book exclusively.'

The American director's face did not change. 'That we can discuss later.'

'I want a commitment now,' Daniel insisted.

'I can't commit to that.'

Impasse. Every instinct told him they had gone as far as they were going. But what if he bailed out Anna and simply got the Robbie Barrell treatment?

'I'll think it over,' he said. He turned towards the door.

Peters' tone sharpened. 'Think it over on the way to the lift, Daniel. We have to move on this.'

As he re-entered the trading floor, Daniel passed Anna going in the opposite direction. She looked uneasy.

When she came back she looked homicidal.

* * *

She sat at her desk, breathing evenly, ignoring the wary glance of her assistant.

So that's what the weekend was about.

The decision had already been made. No wonder Frank had been so keen to reassure her. And she had believed *he* was inept in handling people!

'Peters won't stay over here for ever,' he had told her. 'The Americans know the value of a British senior director in the City. Stick with me, Anna. I'm going to need friends on the board.'

Until his masters demanded otherwise.

She shook her head; not surprised, not surprised at all, but blindingly, furiously *angry*. Then she looked up and caught Daniel watching her, his face impassive.

Oh this is going to be wonderful, she thought. *This is going to be just marvellous.*

'Why'd' you cover that position in the ninety-fours?' Daniel asked.

Glancing at him over her VDU. Anna said coolly: 'It's never wrong to take a profit.'

Daniel snorted. 'It's small change – '

'It's money in the bank.'

'Jesus!' Daniel laughed. 'Let's sell apples from a barrow.'

Anna stared at him as he picked up the phone, stabbing a tab then reaching for a cigarette with his free hand.

'Fred?' he said. 'It's Daniel. Are you in this new seven-year package?' He nodded. 'OK – I'll get back to you.' He put down the phone.

'What's happening? Anna asked.

Daniel raised a hand. 'Just a minute. I'm thinking.' He began to tap rapidly at his keyboard.

Anna looked down at her screen and frowned. 'I don't want any major exposure in synthetics.'

Daniel stopped and sighed. Then he stood up. 'Look,' he said, 'can I talk to you for a moment?'

She watched him circle the end of the octagon and settle himself on the edge of her desk.

'Listen,' he said, bending his head close, 'you're going to be all year digging your way out of this position if you can't commit to some major moves – '

'I don't like the risk.'

He frowned. 'What's risky about this?'

'There's no contingency for any movement in the market,' she said. 'It smacks of one of your spectacular deals.'

'It *works*!'

Anna's eyes hardened. 'It's a goddamn, heat-seeking missile!'

Daniel gasped, shook his head, rose. He *knew* this was going to be impossible. The whole arrangement was a joke.

Anna watched him, unmoving.

He sat down again, glanced at her quickly.

'You've got nice breasts.'

Her eyebrows leapt in shock, and faint amusement.

'More than I can say for you!'

'So – ' Daniel blinked, and it was as if the brief interchange had never happened. 'We won't do it. What do you want to do then, *boss*?'

Anna unbent fractionally. 'Listen, Daniel. I didn't ask to be put in this position.'

His expression soured. 'You've got your sweetheart, Mallory, to thank for that.' He moved away.

'I was totally opposed to this!' Anna snapped angrily at his back.

He dropped into his seat. They eyed each other over the tops of their screens, the air crackling between them like a summer storm.

Daniel looked down at his VDU. He breathed in. At this rate they were going to kill each other in a week. But he *had* got away with the boob crack.

He leaned forward and began to tap at his keyboard.

Anna blinked in surprise as her screen went blank. Then an internal message appeared. It read: I LOVE IT WHEN YOU ABUSE ME. BY THE WAY, I'M NOT BUSY TONIGHT. Abruptly the screen flashed back to the dollar page.

She looked over the top. Daniel was leaning back in his chair, gazing vaguely at the ceiling. His gaze dropped marginally to include her, and an eyebrow lifted.

Anna swallowed a smile.

Skipping neatly between lines of slow-moving traffic, she came towards the car. Daniel took the opportunity to admire her legs, then leaned across and pushed open the front passenger door. She slipped inside and deposited a large, warm-smelling, boxed pizza on the leather padding between the seats.

'I thought you might embarrass me,' Daniel said, switching on the engine. 'Take us somewhere really fancy.'

'Four quid,' Anna pointed out, opening the box and showing it to him. 'It's got everything on it.'

Daniel grinned faintly and indicated that he was moving off. 'Don't misunderstand me. I appreciate it. It's not often a girl buys me dinner. You've bought me two.'

A gap appeared in the traffic. He drove forward.

Anna picked up a slice of pizza. 'You wouldn't know anything about a bunch of balloons floating around in my apartment, would you?'

'Balloons?' Daniel glanced unnecessarily over his shoulder.

'Blue balloons,' Anna nodded. 'About a dozen of them.' She eyed him keenly, until a smirk betrayed him. 'Come on!' she cried. 'I'm dying to know how you got them in there.'

Grinning, he glanced at her. 'No idea at all, eh?'

'Nope. I'm stumped.'

'Well, it's really very simple.' He took a pizza slice she handed him. 'The trick is to blow them up while they're inside and you're outside.

Anna swallowed a mouthful of food. 'You're really very imaginative. And you must have terrific stamina.'

'Helium.' Daniel spoke through his own mouthful.

'Really?' Anna nodded. 'Very clever.'

'But you're right,' Daniel asked, 'I do have terrific stamina.' He caught her glance in the dashboard glow: wry, wary, interested.

Christ, he thought *how quickly can your luck change*?

An obliging, amenable, friendly Anna Schumann was shock enough to his system. An *available* one threatened overload. She had obviously decided on co-operation. Now he wondered if she was the kind of woman who couldn't have a close relationship with a man unless she slept with him.

He sincerely hoped she was.

Pizza demolished, he drew to a halt outside her apartment block and cut the engine. The doorman was late tonight. They looked at each other in silence. Anna's eyes gleamed – with the prospect of acceptance, or last minute dismissal?

Then she turned away and stepped out of the car. 'You'd better leave the key with the doorman,' she said. 'They'll clamp you otherwise.'

Thank you, God.

Smiling, Daniel pulled the key out of the ignition and followed her inside.

Anna opened the door of her flat, Daniel close behind her. She turned on the light and moved down the hallway. Daniel glanced up at the balloons, then shut the door. The sound of a minuet guided him to the living room.

It was a large room, expensively and stylishly furnished, and very feminine. Anna turned from switching on the last of three small table lamps. She had already removed her jacket. 'I don't have any Paderewski,' she said, smiling as she passed him.

'I like Haydn,' he said.

She went into the kitchen. He heard the clink of glasses, and lit a cigarette. Then, having inhaled once, he followed her.

She was mixing cocktails, her back to the door. Her head tilted slightly and he knew she was smiling, acutely aware of him. He looked at the blonde strands fanning the back of her neck, the pink curve of her ear.

Then he stubbed out his cigarette, moved close and took hold of her arm. As he turned her round, her face rose to him. She was still smiling, superb eyes glowing – a look he remembered from the first time they had met, in Mallory's office. A look of triumph.

He bent his head as if to kiss her, and her lips opened. Deliberately, he paused.

Uncertainty flickered across her features.

Then he kissed her.

Thirteen

Daniel woke just after dawn. Anna lay beside him, an arm outflung, the bed sheet tangled about her thighs. In sleep her face looked childlike; washed clean of guile and guilt, teasing and triumph.

Her body was a dream.

Easing away the sheet, Daniel sat up and reached for the cigarette packet on her bedside table. He could not have slept more than three or four hours. Now he felt not tired, but light-headed, his body stretched and strained by pleasureable excess. It had been less a lovemaking than an erotic contest. He had wondered how she would capitulate, grow submissive before merging her desire and his in the act itself.

The answer was, she hadn't.

Every move he made, every stroke, every kiss had been matched, then topped by one of her own; and topped by him again, in a dizzying, exhilarating spiral only exhaustion could end.

He had slept with women who had been demanding in bed; he had slept with women who had given themselves wholly to his pleasure. But, before Anna, he had never slept with a woman who did both. The result was wildly exciting, sometimes awe-inspiring, and faintly disturbing too.

With the dazed air of someone to whom something extraordinary has happened, but which he has yet to assess,

Daniel padded through to the kitchen and glanced in the fridge. He was looking for grapefruit juice, something sharp to clear his throat. Anna clearly spent little time eating at home. Sighing, he shut the fridge door. There had to be something open nearby. He wasn't going to sleep again.

He found his clothes on the living room floor, a set of keys on a table in the hallway.

As he passed the bedroom door again, Anna called out. 'Are you leaving?'

He ducked his head through the doorway. She was half sitting up, gazing sleepily, the sheet over her breasts.

'Getting some breakfast,' he said.

'Get some papers. There's a place a couple of blocks towards Oxford Street.'

He nodded. Then she grinned. 'Hi.'

He grinned back, sliding into the room. 'Hi, yourself.'

She lifted her face to him. He dipped his head and kissed her. As he straightened, the bedsheet slipped to her waist. Her grin broadened as his gaze dropped to her breasts. When he took a deep breath, she chuckled.

'Ten minutes,' he said, and made for the door.

The morning was overcast, slightly chill, a faint wind dislodging waste paper along deserted North Audley Street. Turning up the collar of his suit jacket, Daniel bought milk and orange juice off a passing milk float. A few minutes later he found a newsagent and picked up *The Financial Times*, *Wall Street Journal* and the *Independent*.

As he retraced his steps, he realized his mood had crystallized. He felt tired, and a little empty, and not at all sure what he was doing here. Along the street, on the opposite side, he noticed a payphone. The impulse grew in him as he drew near. Without allowing himself to think about it, he crossed, pushed in a coin and dialled.

Bonnie's voice filled the earpiece. 'This is Bonnie Dever-ill. I'm not here at the moment, but leave me a message and I'll get back to you as soon as I can . . .'

Old emotions churned inside him: disappointment, fear, pain.

Then the answerphone trilled, and he realized he had no idea what to say. 'Hi – it's me,' he started quickly, awkwardly. 'It's Daniel. You there? I just wanted to talk to you – that's all. Just wanted to –'

He stopped, his own inadequacy overcoming him. 'Anyhow – I'll see you –'

He put down the phone, feeling his face burn with stupidity. Did he really expect her to answer a call at six in the morning?

Especially from him.

Now his message would only embarrass her, give her beach god of a boyfriend something to laugh at. Swearing under his breath, he re-crossed the street and hurried on to Anna's flat.

Two miles to the west, Bonnie, wrapped tightly in the dressing gown she had thrown on a moment ago, looked up from her answerphone to the rooftops of Holland Park, just visible through the slatted blinds of her living room. 'Daniel,' she murmured softly, her tone half of pity, half of regret. Then, sighing, she reached down and turned off the machine.

Fourteen

The art gallery was a broad trapezium, all white walls and pine-coloured parquet, with a plateglass panorama of the Broadgate ice rink. The exhibits – exclusively abstract and anaemic – were displayed on huge, white, rectangular panels, hanging from ceiling to knee-height at fifteen-foot intervals; they swayed faintly but disturbingly in the eddies of the crowd.

Against one long wall, the silver-grey eagle head of the Whitney Paine logo was prominent.

Daniel emptied his champagne flute in time to replace it from the tray of a passing waiter. 'I hate these corporate events,' he murmured, his gaze drifting to a pastel blur on his left. 'And these pictures.'

'Ah, come on,' Anna chivvied him. 'You just got to walk twice around the place, eat a few hors d'oeuvres and leave. What's so tough about that?'

She was dressed in pale blue, a nod towards the fact that this early evening, third quarter party was at least partially social in nature. Daniel had made no sartorial concessions; carrying out unpaid PR for Whitney Paine, especially under the eyes of senior management, had never appealed to him.

He glanced up and down the corridor of panels in which he and Anna stood. Two fund managers chatted earnestly at the opposite end; they were otherwise unobserved.

'Listen,' said Daniel, leaning close. 'I've got a better

idea. We could slip away from here, find a quiet place to have dinner . . .'

Anna smiled wryly as his arm hooked hers.

'Maybe drink a little more than we ought to. What do you say?'

'Hmmm . . .' Cocking her blonde head, she considered it. 'Sounds nice.'

'Yeah,' said Daniel, 'but what do you say?'

'I think we should give this an hour.'

Daniel growled in the back of his throat; a sound that snapped off abruptly as Frank Mallory suddenly rounded the end of a panel only a few feet away.

'Shu!' he said at once. Then his eyes dropped to where Daniel still hooked Anna's arm; distaste flickered across his face. In the same instant a tall, fair-haired, elegant woman in her early forties appeared at his side. 'Anna – ' Mallory hurried on smoothly, turning, 'this is my wife, Carla.' As the older woman smiled, he nodded towards Daniel. 'Daniel Pascoe, one of our more flamboyant traders.'

Daniel and Anna smiled their greetings.

Mallory's wife turned pale blue eyes on Daniel. 'Lee Peters thinks highly of you, Daniel,' she said. 'He describes you as a star.'

Daniel made a deprecating gesture, still flattered that the remark should have been made. At the same time he was aware of a slightly more than polite interest in the woman's gaze. She was still attractive; ten years ago she would have been stunning. He wondered if Mallory wasn't alone in marital straying.

'Of course, stars burn out.' Frank added pointedly.

Daniel gave him a blank look. There was a pause.

'Are you enjoying yourself, Anna?' Mallory continued.

She smiled sweetly, her arm – to Daniel's delight – still entwined in his. 'Thank you, Frank. Yes, I am.'

'Anna and Daniel are working together to bring down the losses incurred on the dollar book,' Mallory told his wife. 'They've beaten it down from one hundred million to eighty-one. Pretty good going.'

Mrs Mallory raised her eyebrows appreciatively, her gaze gliding from Anna, dipping to her linked arm and finishing on Daniel. He wondered how much she knew, or cared, about Mallory's dalliances. 'You must both be terribly clever,' she said to Daniel. 'I can't even balance my cheque book.'

'Neither can I,' Daniel smiled.

Mrs Mallory laughed brightly, looking into Daniel's face. Her husband's hand appeared under her elbow. 'You'll excuse us, won't you?' he said, guiding his wife away. There was a hint of regret in her parting smile.

Daniel glanced at Anna, but she was gazing into her champagne flute. She disengaged his arm and he followed her out of the panel corridor into a wider, more crowded area. To one side they glimpsed the Mallorys colliding with Lee Peters and his rather dowdy American academic wife.

They turned in the opposite direction.

'Are you "Shu" to all your friends?' Daniel asked, amused.

'A couple of people call me that,' she said, still not meeting his eyes.

They paused to take fresh champagne glasses from a passing waiter. Anna sipped absently, clearly discomforted by her first meeting with Mallory's wife.

'You and Frank are pretty cool,' Daniel commented. 'You don't think his wife suspects?'

Anna breathed in. 'Daniel,' she said, 'I need time to handle this. Let's not talk about Frank. Not now.'

As Daniel looked at her, she turned away and moved further into the crowd. Daniel grunted and glanced round. He caught sight of Jamie Dunbar, standing alone, gazing blankly at a large, multi-coloured canvas on the long wall.

He moved across to him. 'Jackson Pollock would have a heart attack,' he said.

Jamie glanced up and grinned. As a junior he felt even more out of place here than Daniel did. But before he could say anything, Elana Cimino appeared from the throng.

'*Mister* Pascoe!' she beamed.

Daniel turned and grinned at her as she linked arms, swaying against him. She was wearing a bright red silk dress, over-endowed with frills, which drew considerable attention to her bust, but did little for the rest of her figure.

Jamie frowned at her. 'Can we get you a drink, Elana?' He signalled to a waiter.

'No thanks – I've brought my own.' She hiccupped and covered her mouth. 'I don't drink that shit.' She disentangled herself from Daniel to prise a can of Budweiser out of a voluminous shoulder bag. As she pulled off the top, the waiter arrived.

Jamie took a glass from him. 'Perhaps you should eat something,' he suggested.

Elana chuckled, leaned against Daniel and grinned up at him. 'Where's the chief trader?' she asked.

'Anna?' said Daniel. 'She's around.'

Elana's gaze sharpened. 'You're usually around her.'

'It's just a professional association, Elana.'

'Bullshit!' Elana burst out laughing and pushed herself upright, rocking Daniel back on his heels. 'Just remember, Daniel: you should never sleep with the boss.'

'No?' He glanced round, catching a wary look from Jamie.

'No,' said Elana flatly, and hiccupped again. 'You can sleep with the staff – but not with the boss.'

Daniel nodded sagely, wondering what on earth had happened to Wolfgang Bauer.

The room was at the back of the main gallery space; a small, quiet area, empty but for a large, squat sculpture in black stone. Two low windows opposite the door over-looked a narrow, brick-walled yard, full of trailing plants.

Anna gazed out into it, gripping her empty glass. For a month now she had toyed with the idea of telling Frank Mallory it was all over, knowing that, politically, such an idea was suicidal, at least until the dollar book was straight, and perhaps even after that; the man might still honour his promises. But, emotionally, she longed for clarity.

She had never liked the idea of simultaneous involvement with two men; and two men as close to home, and as mutually antipathetic as Daniel and Frank, imposed an almost intolerable strain. And yet she could see no other way of keeping tabs on Daniel. Pretending a mutual attraction didn't exist would have imposed even greater strains.

A footfall at her back broke into her thoughts. She turned and saw Frank Mallory, smiling warily as he lifted up a bottle of champagne.

She held out her glass to be re-filled. 'I didn't expect to be introduced to your wife,' she said as he finished pouring.

His smile vanished. 'I'm sorry. I hope you weren't embarrassed.'

She blinked slowly. 'I wasn't.'

He filled his own glass and set the bottle down on the

window ledge. 'How are you getting on with Pascoe? You seem quite – relaxed – together.'

Anna felt her chest tighten. Playing this kind of the piggy-in-the-middle game was just the situation she feared. 'We get along fine,' she said.

Mallory raised an eyebrow. 'You see each other socially?'

'Frank.' Anna stared at him. 'It was *your* idea that we run the book together. And, anyway, it's none of your business.'

Mallory blinked, taken aback. 'Forget it,' he said briskly. 'I was just curious.' He waited while she sipped at her champagne. Then his expression softened. She was clearly under strain. He took her arm and drew her towards him. Frowning, she broke away.

'What's wrong?' he said, genuinely surprised.

She glanced towards the open door. 'This is hardly the place, Frank. Your wife's here. There are people everywhere.'

His face stiffened, then he reached past her to put his glass down next to the bottle and take a cigar cylinder from his jacket pocket. Unscrewing it, he glanced out of the window. 'We still OK for Saturday?'

'Sure.' Anna sipped again.

He stared at her. She stared back.

'Fine,' he said. 'I'll pick you up.'

He lit his cigar. She walked past him and out of the room. He inhaled deeply, drawing the warm smoke down into his lungs as if to dispel the chill of his reception. Surely the girl wouldn't be so stupid as to prefer Pascoe to him? She must know he resented having to use the young man as much as she did.

Or professed she did.

Frowning, he moved to the door. He was in time to see

Anna sliding away through the crowd, with Daniel close behind her. They were making for the exit.

Mallory's frown deepened, until he caught Lee Peters' curious glance from several yards across the room. His face lightened immediately, and, snatching a fresh champagne flute, he went to join his boss.

Fifteen

Anna had been busy at the weekend, and Robbie out investigating local hostelries, so Daniel had the unusual experience of a Saturday evening to himself. The result was that he woke before nine on Sunday morning for the first time in years. He decided to celebrate by flying to the Medway towns to pick up groceries and the Sunday papers.

It was nearly eleven when he got back, and he felt in need of company. He went and knocked on Robbie's door. Entering, he found the ex-trader still in bed, the duvet draped over his head. Despite the sunshine pouring through the uncurtained windows, the main light was on.

Robbie shook his head free and opened an eye.

'You slept with the light on,' Daniel pointed out.

'I know,' Robbie grunted. 'I'm afraid of the dark. Always have been.' His other eye opened and squeezed shut again at the day's brilliance. Blindly he reached for the half-finished cigar and booklet that lay on the bedside table. 'What day is it?'

'Sunday,' Daniel told him, and opened a window. As if on cue, church bells echoed distantly.

Robbie dragged himself into a sitting position. 'I like Sundays,' he announced, lighting his cigar. 'Sundays in London. The markets – Brick Lane, Whitechapel . . .' He drew on the cigar and coughed spectacularly. Wincing, Daniel withdrew.

He went down to the kitchen, tossed the wolfhound a

fillet steak from the fridge, and set about grinding coffee beans.

The coffee was percolating when Robbie appeared in the doorway, then lurched on towards the living room. A few minutes later Daniel followed him with two coffees and a glass of orange juice on a tray.

Robbie was standing at the window, gazing at the summer sunlight dancing on the lake. He turned and saw the orange juice. 'I might need something a bit fiercer than that, Daniel,' he frowned. Daniel pushed the glass into his hand. Squinting, the older man sipped, then, as he tasted the vodka, his face brightened. 'Ah – that's not so innocent, is it?'

Grinning, Daniel set down the tray, and then flopped onto the couch and snatched up a sleazier Sunday newspaper.

Robbie drained his glass and remained staring out of the window. 'May have a little enterprise of my own soon, Daniel,' he said at length. 'I found this restaurant . . . hardly a restaurant – an inn – a couple of miles away. It's going downhill; the guy wants to pack it in.' He sucked at his cigar. 'I thought I might try and put something together . . . bit more upmarket; attract the local aristocracy. There's nothing decent out here. I reckon I'd pick it up for change.'

He paused and the sudden glance he gave Daniel contradicted his casual tone.

But Daniel was already looking up. 'You'll be good at that.' He straightened his newspaper. 'Perhaps we could do it together.'

'Yeah?' Robbie grinned hugely. 'Really? Would you want to?' Then he shrugged dismissively and looked away; the young man was humouring him, and he owed him enough already. 'Nah – you're too busy.'

'I could be a sleeping partner.'

Robbie looked back. Daniel was entirely serious. 'Yes, you could.'

He mirrored Daniel's grin.

'The best type to have.'

After breakfast they went out to shift the goats. Over the past six weeks the animals had transformed most of the front lawn from a jungle to a rather skimpy meadow; bald patches were even starting to show. But the gentle sweep down to the lake still resembled veldt. With the help of the wolfhound they left the goats about halfway down, then strolled on to the water's edge, settling on a large log at the end of the jetty.

The noonday sun was hot, discomfort kept at bay by a faint breeze which raised ripples across the water and set the seaplane's floats creaking gently against the jetty's side.

Swishing idly at the reeds with a long stick, Robbie puffed at his cigar and enjoyed a peculiar sense of peace. It wasn't simply the result of Daniel's offer, generous as it was; it was the sense of a deliberate hiatus – a step back to reflect on past mistakes, to gather forces for fresh ventures – the kind of pause that, for the past eleven years, had been the one luxury he hadn't been able to afford.

It was only as he came to this conclusion that he realized Daniel had not spoken a word for almost five minutes. 'You seem pre-occupied, Danny boy,' he prompted.

Daniel prised a stone from the shadow of the log, straightened and tossed it into the water. 'I can't get this girl to make any major moves,' he said heavily. 'We're doing all these penny ante deals. They won't make a dent in our position.'

Robbie toyed with the stick. Whitney Paine was in his past now; he was reluctant to presume an authority that no longer belonged to him. 'You don't need me to tell you what to do,' he said awkwardly.

Daniel turned to him. 'What *would* you do?'

'Come on!' Robbie laughed. 'You're the golden boy. They didn't keep you around because they like the cut of your suit – '

'Robby – ' Daniel's expression was wholly serious. 'What would you do?'

Robbie sighed and stood up. He raised his stick and the wolfhound, slumped at his side, immediately sprang to its feet, muzzle uplifted. Robbie flung the stick a good fifty feet along the lakeside, and the dog bounded after it.

'I've known you too long, Danny boy,' he said, watching the animal go. 'You want me to confirm what you're already thinking.' He turned and looked down at Daniel. 'I'd double my position. You've got a trade figures announcement in a couple of days. Should give the market a shot. Double your position – tough it out.'

Daniel frowned. 'We're talking about another hundred million. She'd never go for it.'

The wolfhound returned with the stick in its mouth. Robbie bent to reclaim it, then flung it away again, this time up the slope towards the house. 'Doesn't have to know,' he said, gazing after the dog. 'Does she?'

He turned again to find Daniel staring at him intently.

Sixteen

'Fuck the deutschmark!'

Daniel swivelled in his chair to catch Elana standing over her screen, fists clenched, eyes blazing.

'What's up, Elana?' Anna asked from the senior trader's desk.

Elana smacked her desktop. 'I just got hit – an hour's work down the toilet!' Breathing in, she raised eyes ceiling-ward. 'I'll *never* touch another Frankfurter.' She glimpsed Wolfgang's look as her eyes dropped again. 'No offence, Wolfgang.'

Anna entered the octagon and bent over Elana's desk as the dark-haired girl sat. 'What went wrong?'

As they began to talk, Daniel glanced at Jamie. The young American was talking rapidly on the phone, eyes glued to his screen. The morning rush hour; a whole weekend's non-trading to make up for and everyone in sight of Daniel was fully occupied.

Leaning forward, he picked up his phone, holding it to the ear away from Jamie and the others. He pressed the Salomon's tab. 'Pascoe at Whitney Paine,' he spoke quietly. 'What's your price in the long bond?' He grunted at the reply and jotted it on a notepad. 'Mark me for fifty million,' he said, and cut the line. He replaced the phone, raised his left hand to his chin and, with his right, scribbled out a deal ticket, which he slipped into his top drawer. Then he yawned, stretched his arms and took the opportunity to glance round the octagon. Anna and Elana were still talking; Jamie was still on the phone. Even Wolfgang at the far end, too far away to overhear, had his head down.

Satisfied, Daniel resumed normal trading.

At one o'clock he went to lunch, strolled along a packed Old Broad Street to Liverpool Street Station and made a call from the first working payphone he found.

'Lennox Mayhew.' The BZW dealer's voice was strained.

'Daniel. What's your price in US bonds – thirty year?'

Lennox sounded surprised. 'What do you want with thirty-year Yankee paper?'

'What's your *price*?' Daniel hissed.

'Ninety-six – '

'I'll take fifty.'

'You got fifty.' Lennox' tone suggested mild insanity in the caller.

Daniel put down the receiver and took a deep breath. He had just surpassed his personal trading capacity by some twenty million dollars. Now he was in clear space – free flying: if this one didn't work out, an awful lot of money, a good part of the bank itself and, least of all, his own job would go merrily down the drain.

He was completely, terrifyingly alone in unknown territory.

Then he thought again and realized that was not quite right.

Tony Eisner had been here before him.

That night he drank alone in the Thames-side cocktail bar. Two girls sat down at the next table, one brunette, one blonde, angular and striking.

The blonde faced him and, as their eyes briefly met, a

look of wry interest, half curious, half encouraging, formed on her face. She read a kind of bravado into Daniel's blank stare; she had, after all, told him to piss off the last time he had attempted communication. But when she glanced away and back again, only to meet the same blank look, her features stiffened, and she turned to talk to her friend.

Miles away, Daniel caught only her look of dismissal, remembered her vaguely from his drink with Jamie and instantly dismissed her as a lost cause. Then his eyes dropped to the Reuters LCD on the table top in front of him.

The green letters read: 'US GOV BOND – DOWN 0.5 – 95.5'

He was up to a hundred and sixty million dollars' worth. Sixty thousand more to pick up throughout the next day's trading, and the first half of Wednesday; the US trade figures would come in the afternoon. At this rate, the longer he left it the cheaper US bonds would get.

But there could be an excellent reason for that.

Daniel drew deeply on the cigarette he held, willing the bitter smoke to swamp the sudden drumming of his heart.

Tough it out, Robbie had said. *Tough it out.*

He signalled to the waiter for another drink.

At noon the following day a tilt in the Eurobond market sent the dealing room into a sudden flurry of activity; phone tabs flashed wildly, screens flickered from page to page; there was a good deal of shouting.

The deutschmark had taken an unexpected lurch downward, provoking a rare bout of near hysteria in Wolfgang. Half the world, it seemed, was shifting to different currencies.

'Daniel!' Anna called over the hubbub, telephone receiver raised. 'I've got Bucklehaus on forty-three – ?

Daniel lifted a hand. He sat back in his chair, feet resting on the top of his Reuters screen; one telephone was draped over his shoulder; he was talking into another. He covered the mouthpiece and shouted back, 'Can you talk to him, please? I've got Carol Teuffel on my shoulder, and O'Halloran in my ear!'

Anna nodded and sat down.

'OK,' Daniel continued his call, 'I'll mark you for ten in the twenty year.' He cut the line and pressed another flashing tab. 'In the franc? Ninety-eight. You buying or prospecting?' He nodded. 'OK.' The tab went dark; there were no other calls on the screen.

Daniel rose in his chair. Anna was still talking. The lull seemed only to have touched him.

He pressed the tab for Credit Suisse First Boston. 'What's your price in the long bond?' He grunted at the reply, scribbling it on his pad. Ninety-four; down a point and a half on yesterday's close. He needed thirty million more, but he no longer dared make the calls from here. 'I'll get back.'

He cut the line and stood, arching his back, and catching Anna's eye. 'I'm going to take a leak.'

Still on the phone, she nodded then watched him pad towards the door. The thought that he looked tireder, more tense than usual crossed her mind; he had not slept with her for almost a week. Her call ended and an internal tab immediately flashed. She picked it up; it was query for Daniel from settlements; a deal ticket requested but not received.

'No, he's away from his desk,' Anna said. 'Hold on.' Standing, she moved round the octagon, trailing the telephone wire after her. She scanned Daniel's desk. 'I don't see anything, Wallace. I'll remind him, OK?'

As the line went dead, her eye was caught by Daniel's scribbled note to himself. 'T bond 94%.' Her brow furrowed momentarily. Why was Daniel interested in US Treasury bonds? They had agreed to concentrate on securities to grab all the short term profit going, not government bonds that took at least seven years to mature.

She became aware of Patrick Skill trying to attract her attention to another call. Filing away her curiosity, Anna went back to her desk.

Daniel glanced up at the clock. Six pm. The London market was winding down, and Wall Street was quiet, perhaps in part due to depressed US bond prices. But all the dealers he needed to reach would be at their desks until six thirty. He had already selected a suitable payphone – the nearest – in London Wall; speed now counted more than caution. He got up, pulling on his jacket. Anna looked up.

'I have to go for half an hour,' he said.

She frowned. 'You OK?'

'Sure.' It took an effort to smile easily. 'Why don't I meet you around seven thirty – at the plane?' Before she could reply he bent and scribbled something on his notepad. Tearing off the sheet, he folded it in two and handed it to her over the screens.

'Take care of this, would you?'

He winked, picked up his cigarettes and turned towards the door.

Anna opened the note. It bore a large pencilled heart, pierced by an arrow. But when she glanced up with a wry smile, Daniel was no longer in the room.

★ ★ ★

An hour later the trading floor was deserted, screens dark. In her office, Anna picked up her document case, switched off the desk lamp and went out into the main hallway. Passing two elderly female cleaners, she walked to the far end and turned down a narrow corridor. She paused outside a door marked SECURITY: OPERATIONS and stepped inside.

The room was small and windowless. Banks of monitors occupied one entire wall, giving numerous black and white views of the bank's interior: entrances, exits, hallways, trading floor. Elaborate recording equipment stood to one side.

A young black girl in a security uniform swivelled in a central chair, her broad face breaking into a surprised smile. 'Good evening, Miss Schumann.'

'Hi, Beth,' Anna smiled back. 'Could I get the voice records, please, on Daniel Pascoe's position?'

The girl turned to lift a clipboard off the small desk in front of her. She handed it to Anna with a biro. 'Some dispute over a trade,' Anna explained, signing. 'Like to clear it up.'

The girl got up and went to a corner cabinet. Opening a drawer, she thumbed through a file, took out a tape cassette and brought it back to Anna. She chuckled. 'This guy's racing up the charts!'

Anna looked at her. 'What do you mean?'

'Mr Mallory asked for Mr Pascoe's voice records only yesterday.'

'Is that so?'

A slightly raised eyebrow was all that betrayed Anna's considerable surprise. Checking Daniel's phone deals had been a momentary whim – a sop to a teasing sense of unease. But if Frank had shared the same suspicion it was a good deal more serious. And why hadn't she been informed?

She had planned to scan the tape briefly at home, or early next morning.

She opened her case and slipped the cassette inside.

Now she would go back to her office and check through it immediately.

'Hi,' Daniel grinned with undisguised relief. 'I thought I was being stood up.'

He held the taxi door open as Anna stepped out. 'I was delayed.' she said. 'I'm sorry.'

His grin wavered as she paid the driver. She seemed distant, preoccupied.

They crossed the pavement and entered an alleyway between tall buildings.

'Everything OK?' Daniel asked.

'I need to talk to you,' Anna said.

'Well, talk to me over dinner.' Daniel skipped ahead, unlocking a wooden door at the alley's end. Steps led down to a pontoon bridge and a floating jetty where the Cessna rocked in the reflected glow of sunset.

'I've got a house guest I'd like you to meet,' Daniel called back to her. He appeared almost boyishly excited. 'He's a *terrific* cook.'

Anna paused, the knowledge of what she had gleaned from Daniel's phone tapes a tight knot in her chest. It would be easy to be angry, easy to explode, but this was neither the time or place.

Daniel held the alley door open, beckoning her forward. 'And we're almost an hour late!'

Seventeen

Daniel felt the exuberance of the condemned man; or how he imagined a man would feel receiving such a sentence at the end of a particularly prolonged and nerve-wracking trial. He had succeeded in doubling his position minutes short of the close of trading. Two hundred million dollars' worth of Whitney Paine's liquidity tied to the fortunes of the American government, on his personal authority alone. The thought was so staggering it was hard to suppress the bubble of hysterical laugher.

He realized he had never quite believed he could succeed. Rumours, computer checks, a sharp eye on the flow of deal tickets he had deliberately reduced to a trickle; any one of a dozen separate things could have scuppered him. Getting this far was an achievement in itself.

And now every passing hour compounded his success – or a catastrophe so gigantic it beggared description. All he had to do was survive for eight short hours tomorrow.

Tough it out, Danny boy, tough it out.

He glanced across the cabin at Anna, suddenly and guiltily aware that he had hardly spoken a word to her since taking off. But familiar landmarks were creeping up ahead in the gathering dusk. He would be home in minutes.

Neither Anna nor Robbie had been forewarned of the other's presence this evening. The thought of them sparring together gave Daniel a faintly malicious pleasure. He had no doubt who would win.

They were over the twin oasts of the house before he realized something was wrong. The lake was dark.

Anna glanced at him. 'What's the problem?'

'Had some lights put in.' Daniel frowned, pulling the plane into a turn. 'Probably just a fuse gone.'

Unease blossomed as he touched down, taxiing slowly to the end of the jetty. There were no lights in the house, either. He cut the motor and climbed out to secure the plane. The whole place was in silence; a wind ruffled the water.

'Robbie!' Daniel shouted, moving along the jetty.

'Robbie Barrell?' Anna asked, coming after him.

'That's right,' Daniel flung over his shoulder. If the old bastard had got pissed and sunk into a stupor . . .

'Robbie!' he shouted again.

The wolfhound greeted them on the edge of the newly-shorn lawn. 'Come on, boy.' Daniel bent over it, smoothing its dark head. 'Show me where the old devil's got to.'

To his surprise the dog turned away from the house and bounded back towards the lake. Frowning, Daniel retraced his steps.

'What is it?' Anna called.

'I don't know.'

Nearing the water, the wolfhound broke away from the path and plunged into long grass. Daniel hurried after it, hearing Anna's footsteps behind him. In the growing twilight he almost collided with an old fence post. As he clutched at it, he saw the empty whisky glass balanced on the top.

'Oh shit – '

He ran now, feeling panic, but there were only two or three yards to go.

Robbie's body made a nest in the tall grass.

He lay curled on his side, knees drawn up to his chest, hands tucked against his chin, as though shielding himself against the cold. He *was* cold, Daniel discovered as he dropped to his knees and pressed fingers against the man's neck and wrist – deathly cold.

Anna loomed behind him. 'Oh my God,' she whispered.

'Robbie – ' Daniel murmured softly, as though afraid of intruding. Then his fingers moved from wrist to hand, squeezing the ex-trader's fingers, and he spoke more boldly, almost chiding. 'For God's sake, Robbie!'

He stood in front of the house, watching two ambulance men close the rear doors of their vehicle, walk to the cab and climb inside. The engine started and the ambulance pulled away slowly along the uneven driveway, full head beams bouncing. It was nearly eleven o'clock and very dark.

Daniel waited until the lights had disappeared.

They had found Robbie's stick, tangled in reeds a couple of feet from where he had collapsed. In all likelihood he had been throwing it for the dog, stretching across a marshy spot; the earth had been damp under his head.

After eleven years of nervous strain, alcohol and chemical abuse, his heart had chosen this moment to rebel. There was no evidence that he had suffered more than the briefest of agonies.

Daniel turned and went indoors. In Robbie's bedroom he assembled the man's few personal items – some letters, a photograph of his ex-wife, his trading certificate – and placed them carefully in a suitcase with the few clothes, mostly old and worn, that Robbie had kept; he had burnt all his business suits, with evident relish, a week after moving in.

Daniel closed the case and locked it, and was invaded suddenly by an overwhelming tiredness. It was the first sensation he could acknowledge for the past two hours. From the instant before he had glimpsed Robbie's body until now, he had been gripped by an extraordinary blankness, a deadness of feeling behind which thoughts buzzed and emotions stirred, but distantly as though they belonged to someone else. He wondered if it was a symptom of shock.

Two bodies now – Tony Eisner's sprawled across a boardroom floor, Robbie's curled on damp earth. And how many bust relationships? He and Bonnie, Robbie and Sheila . . .

This wasn't a game. There was no *fun* in this; these were whole lives, shot to pieces, run ragged, tossed aside. And for what?

For what?

He shut the case and turned. Anna stood in the open doorway, watching him.

He drew in breath. 'He was coming around. He was easing himself off the booze and the coke.' He shrugged awkwardly. 'I think he was happy . . .'

Anna's gaze softened; she reached out to touch his arm. 'I'm sorry, Daniel. I'm really sorry.'

He shook his head, swallowed. Then he looked at her. 'What was it you wanted to say?'

'What?'

'You wanted to talk to me about something.'

'Oh.' Anna nodded faintly, then shook her head. 'Don't worry. That can wait.'

Eighteen

Anna requested and got her appointment with Lee Peters at ten thirty the next morning, the first lull of the day.

The stocky American was standing at his window, looking down through the blinds, as she entered. He turned and smiled. 'Hello, Anna.' He indicated a chair. 'Have a seat. What's up?'

Grave-faced, Anna closed the door on Peters' secretary.

Peters' smile broadened. 'Do I need to have a seat as well?'

'I'm afraid so, Lee,' Anna said, sitting.

But he remained standing, gazing at her expectantly until her apparent resolve wavered, her eyes dropped.

'I . . . er . . .'

Recognizing, and intrigued by her unease, Peters spoke quietly. 'Begin at the beginning.'

Anna breathed in, straightening. 'I've discovered something which might jeopardize the bank's position. And I realize I can't ignore it: it's my responsibility.'

Peters' brow furrowed slightly. 'You're being rather cryptic.'

'Yes – I am,' Anna agreed. She paused and glanced away. 'Well, put simply, Daniel Pascoe has taken a massive position in treasuries, without my knowledge. Our exposure, combined with what we inherited from Eisner, is way beyond my discretion.'

The senior director turned again to the window, silent

for a moment. 'You say, without your knowledge,' he said. 'Then how do you know?'

'I requested the voice records. I sensed something was up.'

Peters glanced back at her. 'Have you challenged Pascoe? What does he say?'

Anna shook her head. 'No, I haven't. The GNP figures are due later today. I think he's expecting an up-turn. He's doubled his position, probably hoping to make a killing.'

Peters' gaze sharpened behind his spectacles. 'How do you view the position?'

'The productivity figures, or Pascoe's bond purchases?'

'The GNP figures.'

'The market's looking for an up-turn.'

The telephone on Peters' desk trilled softly. He ignored it. 'What will you do?' he asked. 'He's your dealer – you're the chief trader.'

Anna hesitated. She had diffused her personal anger at Daniel's deceit, not least as a result of the events of the previous evening. What concerned her much more was that she had been forced to expose herself to senior management. If she disowned Daniel now it would be a tacit admission of her managerial incompetence; if she validated his moves it would undermine every working principle she had ever avowed. But she also prided herself on her realism.

'I'd be inclined to run with it as well,' she said flatly.

Peters' look was steely. 'You wouldn't cut and run?'

'No. If Pascoe's correct we have the opportunity to clean out this position. We'd have an even book. If he's wrong – our position won't deteriorate that much over the day.' In other words, quick selling should contain the loss, and Daniel's salary would be an early economy.

Peters' expression was thoughtful as he absorbed the

implications. 'Are you going to advise Mallory about this?' he asked.

'Frank already knows,' said Anna.

The senior director registered obvious surprise. 'You don't say?'

'He requested the voice records a day ahead of me.'

'Did he?'

'Yes; but what's significant,' Anna went on, 'is that he's said nothing. Not to me. Not to Pascoe. I assume not to you, either.'

Peters rocked slightly on his toes, his eyes on the window again, his lack of comment only confirming Anna's suspicion.

Get out of that, Frank, she thought.

Then Peters turned to her. 'You're the chief trader,' he said firmly. 'The discretion lies with you: and your judgement.'

Anna blinked. Was that a statement of confidence or a threat? 'This goes rather beyond my discretion,' she said.

Peters shook his head. 'Not since you've acquainted me with it. I'll support you if and when it comes necessary.'

Only slightly mollified, Anna stood up.

'Pascoe has a certain ability – a nose,' the director went on. 'Follow it. That's the best I can tell you.'

Anna hesitated. It was clearly the only consolation she would find here. 'Thank you,' she said.

Peters smiled thinly.

Anna turned and left. Outside, she thought, *He knew – he was surprised at Frank, but not at Daniel – he expected something like this.*

And, if that were so, what had he expected of her?

★ ★ ★

Tearing open his second cigarette packet of the morning, Daniel glanced up at the clock – a minute before noon – and then back at his Reuters screen. It read: 'US T BOND DOWN 93:31/32.'

As he watched, the price dropped half a point.

He took a deep breath, drawing a finger across his mouth, feeling his heart jump in his chest.

Four hours. Just four more hours.

Two floors above him, alone in his office, Frank Mallory sat with his feet on his desk, watching the same screen. His expression was one of quiet satisfaction. Another two point drop should do it. A personal intervention on the trading floor, rows, confusion, but just enough time to recoup the worst losses, and Pascoe would be out on his ear. Anna would scream, of course, but that wouldn't last. Not with the personal backing of the director who had saved the bank's bacon – saved it from wideboys and thick-eye specialists like Pascoe and Barrell.

The City was changing, the lessons of Big Bang painfully being applied. There was a place for the older, more urbane, more civilized values, after all: values that meant nothing to a petty shark like Pascoe.

But that was something the young man was about to learn.

No less nervous than Daniel, Anna ordered a salad lunch at her desk, picked at it for over half an hour, then tossed it largely uneaten into her wastebin.

She had done little all day, attention strung between the dollar page and Daniel, who looked increasingly drawn, wreathed in a perpetual blue cloud of cigarette smoke. She had deliberately distanced herself from him, sensing the tension that radiated from him in almost visible waves.

But it was, of course, the five minutes she chose to duck out of the room when all hell broke loose.

She heard the buzz as soon as she re-entered. Several dealers were on their feet, staring at the green Reuters strip high on the wall. Phones were flashing everywhere.

'Jesus!' Elana Cimino exploded. 'The guy's crazy!' She was standing, too, a phone in each hand.

'What happened?' Anna asked her.

Elana turned to her, eyes wide with disbelief. 'The US Treasury Secretary just held a press conference. He said he doesn't mind if the dollar drops another couple of points!'

'What's the market doing?'

Elana laughed. 'Falling like a fucking brick!'

Anna rushed to her desk. On the Reuters screen the bond price was flashing 92:31/32 – half a point down in the few moments she had been out of the room. Two more points and she could forget a recovery today; forget her own job, too, not to mention her future. She glanced up. The dollar desk was empty.

'Where's Daniel?' she snapped at Jamie.

He looked up from a call, pointing. 'The loo – '

Another wave of gasps, groans, ironic laughter rippled across the room. Anna's eyes fell.

A further half point had dropped off the bond price.

She rushed across the trading floor, out into the main hallway, down three doors to the gents and straight inside.

Splashing water in his face, Daniel looked up in surprise from a wash basin. Behind him a senior settlements manager zipped hurriedly, flashed Anna a pale smile and exited.

'You'd better get out of here – we got a problem,' she

gasped. 'The market's falling. The long end's down a point and a half.'

Daniel reached for a paper towel. 'Yeah – so?'

Anna's gaze hardened. 'Listen, Daniel. I don't have time to screw around. You're running a two million dollar position – '

His face dropped. 'Wait a minute . . . How . . . ?'

She cut across him, 'Never mind how. I *know* OK? We got to move fast; this could kill us. Come *on*!'

They left at a half run.

'What did the Fed say?' Daniel asked.

'He made some remark about a weaker dollar – everyone reacts – the usual panic.'

It was evident as soon as they reached the floor. They weaved between a forest of standing figures, all eyes glued to the Reuters strip; tabs flashed, telephones chimed in every direction.

'How did you know the position I'm running?' Daniel said.

'I requested the voice records.'

'Oh, that's nice.'

'No worse than having me followed.'

He caught the sting in her voice. Then she left him, crossing to her own desk.

Daniel started at his screen. The bond price was down another half point.

'Everything's going sub aqua,' said Jamie.

'The GNP figures,' Anna called, 'they come at four – right?'

Daniel turned to the clock. A moment after three.

'Can we live that long?' Jamie asked.

Anna swore under her breath.

'I know what you're thinking,' Daniel told her. 'Sell the position now – '

She shook her head. 'We're going to get massacred.'

Daniel raised his hand. 'Listen, listen, we're not. Just another hour. I'm convinced.'

He could see her slipping away; whatever had made her trust him this far was fading. She was still shaking her head. 'We're going to feel the heat long before then.'

Daniel stared at her. 'We *have* to run with this!'

Anna glanced down at her screen. 'It just dropped another point!'

He did not dare look himself, did not dare shift his gaze from her, willing her confidence with all the force he could muster.

She closed her eyes, mouth tightening. '*Give* me the GNP figures, now.' It was a harsh whisper, a prayer.

And something clicked in the back of Daniel's mind.

He snatched up the phone, stabbed the BZW tab. 'Is Lennox there? What – where? For how long? *Shit!* Where is this meeting?' He nodded. 'Right, thanks. No – never mind.' Slamming down the receiver, he grabbed his jacket.

'Where are you going?' Anna cried.

He was already moving away. 'I've got an idea. I've got to talk to Lennox. He's in a meeting with the Bank of England; they won't put any calls through.'

She was staring at him in disbelief.

'Don't do *anything*!' he called across the room. 'Give me thirty minutes – '

Then he was gone.

Nineteen

A taxi slid into the kerb as Daniel came running through the entrance lobby. Inside a young woman passenger fumbled in her purse. Rushing across the pavement, Daniel yanked open the taxi's door, grabbed her arm and pulled her bodily out.

'What the hell – ' she cried.

Daniel sprang inside. 'I'll pay – whatever,' he snapped at the driver. 'Bank of England, *now*!' He slammed the door.

Five minutes later, twenty pounds poorer, he was racing up a wide marble staircase, footsteps echoing in the high-ceilinged space. At the top a broad hallway extended cavernously. A few yards down a pair of tall, dark, varnished doors were guarded by a middle-aged, female commissionaire sitting at a desk. She watched impassively as Daniel panted to a halt in front of her.

He nodded at the doors behind her. 'I have to talk to Mr Lennox Mayhew.'

'That's not possible,' the woman said stiffly. 'I'm sorry. I cannot disturb this meeting under any circumstances.'

Daniel took a deep breath, pulled his wallet from his jacket pocket and flashed the Whitney Paine Security card that bore his photograph. 'Alright; I'm Daniel Pascoe with the Department of Trade and Industry. Division of Investigators. Get him out here or I'll cite you for obstruction!'

The woman stared at him a moment, then, sniffing, she

stood up and went to the doors. 'You could have said so straightaway,' she murmured, and disappeared inside.

Sighing, Daniel moved away down the hallway. His whole body seemed to be prickling with sweat, sparks flashing behind his eye balls.

The tall doors opened and shut with a dull thump.

Daniel turned and saw the commissionaire with an angry-looking Lennox Mayhew. Tall, lean, with boyish features, though six years Daniel's senior, he strode over briskly.

'Daniel? What the hell is this?'

'Jesus, Lennox, I'm sorry. I have to talk to you.' He caught the other's arm, leading him further from the commissionaire's desk.

'Make it bloody quick, Daniel.'

Daniel lowered his voice. 'I have to know the US trade figures.'

Lennox frowned. 'In a couple of hours we'll all know them.'

'No – no.' Daniel shook his head. 'I have to know *now*. You remember a year ago you were screwing that girl at the Federal Reserve? We had the CPI figures the night before they were published – '

'For *Chrissakes*, Daniel!' Lennox hissed, and glanced back over his shoulder. Then he leaned closer, dropping his voice. 'You're out of your mind . . . In any event, I don't even know if she's there any more.'

Daniel closed and opened his eyes. He breathed in deeply. Then his hand slapped against his thigh. 'Could you fucking *try*, Lennox?' he cried.

Across the hallway the commissionaire looked up from her desk. Lennox' frown deepened. 'This'll cost you, Daniel,' he said after a moment. 'I can't even begin to tell you how much.'

It was Lennox who persuaded the commissionaire to find them an ante room with a phone.

Daniel stood with head bowed, eyes shut while Lennox made the call.

'Thanks for your help,' Lennox said finally. 'That's splendid news.'

Daniel opened his eyes as he put down the phone.

Lennox' face was expressionless. 'She left eight months ago, Daniel. She's happily married, expecting her first baby.' He cocked an eyebrow. 'That help you at all?'

He ran.

Heedless between sharp-braking cars, blaring horns.

No sign of a taxi – solid traffic; pedestrians blocking every clear path.

He saw a payphone, pushed into the cubicle an instant before a disgruntled pinstripe, snatched up the phone.

And stopped.

Thoughts churned so fiercely across the surface of his mind they felt like electric froth. Formless sparks. Nothing connected. The only certainty was an abyss, deepening, widening on every side.

And now, finally, he understood why Eisner had done what he had. Not from fear – even sheer, mind-numbing nervous terror – he could experience that a dozen times a week; it was something deeper, more essential. It was a failure of instinct – the instinct that tracked a path through a world as capricious as the market, the gut feeling which said, 'Do this, not that', on minimal information, or sometimes none at all.

Without that there was nothing. You could go through the motions – for weeks, months, perhaps even years. But the first important deal would bring you straight back to the abyss – or the obscene crash of a gun in the early City morning.

He wouldn't do that; he couldn't. But he wouldn't back out, either.

By an effort of will he withdrew from the muddle of thought, the cold current of fear. He let them sink below the surface of his mind.

Half in a dream, he pushed a coin into the machine, dialled Anna's direct line.

'Anna Schumann – '

'It's Daniel.'

'So what did Lennox say?'

And in that instant he knew he had reckoned without one factor: he could fight this all the way himself, but he could not win without Anna. If he lied to her, she would know. If he didn't, he would place more trust in her than he had ever done with anyone professionally; perhaps even privately, too.

'Daniel?' she called.

He closed his eyes. 'No dice,' he said. 'Lennox couldn't help. But it doesn't matter. This market's going to turn – One thousand per cent.'

'How do you know?'

'I *know*.'

Her silence made him grip the phone.

'Daniel – it's just dropped another point.'

'OK, OK.' He sighed, turning in the cubicle, knowing he had been lucky to push her this far, knowing the eighth floor must have got wind of the position by now. 'Are you getting pressure from upstairs?'

'Damn right!'

'Give me five minutes,' Daniel snapped 'Two. I'm on my way – '

'Daniel, I'm *really* putting my arse on the line here. If this goes down, we all go down.'

'Don't do anything; I'll be back!'

He slammed down the phone, turned.

And ran.

Standing at her desk, Anna replaced her receiver and looked up straight into the angry eyes of Frank Mallory.

'Well?' he said.

'I hold the discretion here,' she said flatly.

'I want you to liquidate this position now.' His voice was low, and serious, but heads were lifting around the room. Public clashes involving senior management were rare enough to merit attention; rumours of Daniel's unauthorized position were spreading fast.

Opposite them Jamie, all ears, felt-tipped a gallows onto his Reuters screen.

'I'm running this desk, Frank . . .' Anna's hands were on her hips, eyes glittering.

'Until such time as *I* override you,' Mallory snapped. 'This position is deteriorating by the minute. Sell it!'

'It's going to recover – '

Mallory pointed at the Reuters screen. 'I want you to liquidate, right now!'

Anna flinched visibly, but did not move.

Mallory leaned closer, his voice sharpening to a hiss. 'You were brought in here to run a cautionary position, instead of which you let Pascoe take a two hundred million dollar flyer!'

Anna blinked, refusing to be intimidated. She spoke calmly. 'Frank, you've been aware of this position at least as long as I have. You said nothing, expecting Pascoe to come unglued so you could fire him.'

His angry expression faltered. 'You're mad . . .' To be replaced instantly by one of astonished belief. 'Are you really going to carry the can for him?'

'No one's carrying the can,' said Daniel. 'The GNP figures are going to be way up.'

Mallory spun round.

Daniel's face was bright red, shiny with sweat, his jacket hanging open. With the now undisguised attention of the whole room, he walked through the octagon and rounded on Anna's position.

Mallory straightened. 'How could you possibly know that?'

'Never mind,' Daniel said. 'I know.'

He swapped a tense glance with Anna. Seeing it, Mallory's temper finally erupted. 'You're both on the line here,' he cried, and stabbed a finger at Daniel. 'You've dealt beyond your limit, and *you* – ' he turned, scathingly, on Anna, 'you have failed to monitor the situation. This room was safer with a lush like Robbie Barrell in control!'

Daniel did not pause to think. His left hand grabbed Mallory's arm, jerking him round; his right hand bunched, swung and struck Mallory's jaw with a whiplike crack. Eyes bright with shock, the director staggered past Anna, crashing across her desk and thumping his head against the Reuters screen.

The room went silent.

With a gasp, Mallory pushed himself upright. A wedge of grey hair dropped across his forehead. He turned to Daniel, fingering the red weal on his jaw. 'You're finished here, Pascoe.'

'No.' Daniel shook his head, snarling the words. 'Not until I've squared this position. *Then* I'm finished – yes. But on *my* terms. We made a deal – you wanted a even book, I'm going to get you an even book.' He jerked a finger at Anna. '*We* are. Then I'm out. Now leave me the fuck alone to get on with it!'

Mallory's wounded gaze flickered towards Anna. Her face was set; shocked but unyielding. If he had hoped for any support there, he had left it too long. Her cold stare offered him nothing.

High on the eighth floor, Lee Peters glanced at his wristwatch, rose from behind his desk and crossed to a small Sony TV in the corner of his office. Switching it on, he returned to his desk to watch.

A newscast was reaching the last few items.

'. . . And also from America,' said the young, blonde newscaster, 'some good news for Wall Street. Trade figures just released show an unexpected six point rise in the United States' gross national product – a two and three quarter per cent increase on February's figures. The announcement prompted an immediate up-swing in the money markets, and in bond and share prices. Reporting from Washington, Jane Keys . . .'

Peters reached for a remote control on his desktop and killed the sound. Drawing in breath, he sat back in his chair, momentarily thoughtful.

Then he leaned forward and pressed the intercom. 'Alice,' he told his secretary, 'get me the security department, will you?'

Twenty

The whole trading floor was on its feet, eyes fastened on the green Reuters strip, the mood tense and jubilant.

Anna stood at Daniel's side.

'US T', the strip read, '95:01/16.'

'We've got to see ninety-eight . . .' Daniel hissed.

It stopped at 97:15/16.

Daniel bunched his fist. 'Come on, come *on*!'

'OK.' Anna glanced at him. 'We could go now. We'd be in the black.'

Daniel raised a restraining hand. 'Just hold on, hold on; I want to see another half point . . .'

Anna drew in breath as a minute passed, two.

Jamie bent over his screen. He thumbed out the felt-tipped gallows.

Beneath it the bond price bumped to 98:01/16.

The trading floor's roar was audible in the entrance lobby.

Daniel and Anna swapped a smile as fierce as it was brief.

Then Daniel was diving for his desk.

'OK, let's go – let's clean this position out!'

Jamie was already on the phone. 'Carol Teuffel – forty-four,' he snapped. 'Bucklehaus on forty-six.'

Daniel snatched up his phone, thumbed a tab. 'Carol? In the ten year? Ninety-eight . . . OK. Good; I'll mark you for ten.' His hand reached for a ticket and pen, scribbled:

'Bank of Canada – 10 million.' He cut the line, thumbed another tab.

Opposite him, Anna was speaking into one phone, another on her shoulder. 'Levon, you're done.' She covered the mouthpiece and caught her assistant's eye. 'Patrick – coffee? Very black, very strong.'

Patrick nodded, and left.

'Your size, sir!' Daniel cried. 'Twenty you're sold!'

The room descended into hubbub.

And within an hour was quiet again.

The market was moving on, its electronic storm drawn by the advancing day towards Wall Street, leaving a debris of crumpled memos, piled up deal tickets, discarded plastic coffee cups – and the weary occupants of the Whitney Paine octagon.

Anna had been waiting for Daniel to move, but when it happened it was a jolt.

The look they exchanged, as he stood and pulled on his jacket, was long and thoughtful, a measure of the last traumatic twenty-four hours; and of the previous weeks of sparring, plotting and unexpected intimacy. And, she wondered, with what conclusion? She had given him more than she had ever intended to, and she knew he had, finally, respected that, and her.

But did it change anything?

She rose, and approached him around the end of the octagon, aware of the eyes of Jamie, Elana, even Wolfgang, on both of them. 'Running out on me, Pascoe?' she said, folding her arms.

Daniel scooped a handful of papers from his open drawer and dropped them into his wastebin. He seemed distant, detached. 'The book's straight,' he said simply. 'That's what we set out to do.'

She couldn't hide her frown. 'Is that all that matters here? The book?'

He glanced up at her, as if surprised she should suggest anything else, and she did not know which was more wounding: the surprise itself, or his desire to feign it.

'Yes,' he said. 'Anyhow,' the ghost of a smile surfaced as he flexed his right hand, 'I think my relationship with the management is strained.'

Anna ignored the joke. 'We've got an even book. We can start with a fresh slate – '

'No.' His interruption was harsh, and final.

'What about us?' Elana Cimino said. 'The team?'

Daniel turned to her. She looked at him, open-faced, over a Diet Coke; her jaw flexed on half-forgotten chewing gum. An unconscious parody of herself. Behind her Wolfgang stood with Teutonic calm.

Daniel would miss their daily contests. For the first time he sincerely hoped that Wolfgang was giving the dark girl all she wanted. 'Elana,' he told her, 'wherever you are, it'll be a great team.'

She mirrored his faint grin.

Jamie, ex-aide, drinking partner and occasional conscience, simply looked glum. Daniel gave him a broad wink.

Then he turned back to Anna. His expression softened; it contained admiration, warmth and genuine regret. 'Careful how you fly it,' he said softly.

Then he picked up his cigarettes, pocketed them and walked out of the room.

Aware of too many eyes on her, Anna straightened,

unfolding her arms. 'OK,' she said, suddenly brisk. 'Let's make money.'

Standing at his office window, Lee Peters reached across his desk and picked up the trilling phone.

It was Frank Mallory, flustered and indignant. 'Lee – you're aware of events this afternoon?'

Peters lifted a blind and gazed down onto the street in front of Whitney Paine

'Yes, Frank, I am,' he said calmly. 'Fully aware.'

'A flagrant miscarriage of procedure on Pascoe's part,' Mallory ranted. 'A massive exposure without my consent, or that of the chief trader . . .'

Peters watched Daniel emerge from the overhang of the building and step up to the kerb to hail a taxi.

'. . . I feel the only course open to us is to let Pascoe go,' Mallory continued. 'In the best interests of the bank. In fact, Lee, I'm going to fire him.'

'Are you, Frank?' said Peters.

A taxi halted beside Daniel. He climbed inside and was wafted away, without a single look back.

'I think,' Peters added, 'you may be too late.'

Two floors below, Mallory frowned as the line went dead. Recalling Peters' number, he found it engaged. Puzzled, he rose from the boardroom table, his afternoon shadow falling across the lighter, fresher French polish that marked Eisner's departure.

Had Lee already dealt with Pascoe? Mallory would have expected to be informed, but he had been with the nurse, having his jaw examined. He fingered it now as he walked out of the board room and down the corridor to his office. It was still bloody painful. Even in the bear garden of the trading floor, physical assaults on senior management were beyond the pale. Even an American like Peters must have appreciated that.

And as for Anna . . . He wondered how long she had been sleeping with Pascoe. From the first month, the first fortnight, the first week . . . ?

Calculating, faithless bitch. He'd like to see how long *she* would last without his protection.

He reached the small reception area that contained his secretary's desk, nodding to the petite blonde behind it, who smiled sheepishly.

He grasped his door handle. It refused to turn.

'What the hell's wrong with this door?'

The secretary blinked at him, a blush rising from her upturned collar. 'The security people came by fifteen minutes ago, Mr Mallory.' She coughed awkwardly. 'They changed the locks.'

Mallory stared at her in blank disbelief.

'What?' he said.

Twenty-one

He had not felt such a blankness since the night of Robbie
Barrell's death. But this wasn't the blankness of despair; it
was closer to the emotional exhaustion that followed a week
of manic dealing, multiplied by some extraordinary factor.
A feeling of having stretched every nervous sinew well
beyond breaking point, beyond even his ability to register
strain any more.

And yet a sense of loss remained. He had just committed
his own form of suicide – a form as dramatic and as final as
Tony Eisner's – only much more satisfying because it beat
the system at its own game. A system that maimed and
killed its most efficient exponents. But *he* had won! *He* had
walked away.

Then why this lingering emptiness?

In the gathering dusk, he had just walked heedlessly past
the payphone in St Katharine's Dock when the answer
came to him. He had not even thought of phoning Bonnie.

Her memory brought a stirring of guilt, a pang that
should have hurt, but didn't. And not because of exhaustion, not because his mind had simply been too occupied
with other thoughts, but simply because her hold on him
had gone, had moved gradually but irretrievably, into the
past.

Leaving what?

'Hi, Pascoe.'

In the gloom of the landing stage he had not even glanced

at the seaplane's cockpit. As he did so, a switch clicked and the glow of the instrument panel threw a familiar face into relief.

'What took you so long?' Anna asked.

Daniel pulled open the door, an absurd light-headedness overtaking him. The girl's face was glowing; she was grinning from ear to delicious ear.

'I took a walk,' he said, dazed. 'I needed some air.' Her smile finally became irresistable. 'Aren't you supposed to be somewhere else?'

She shrugged. 'Depends how you look at it. The book's straight. That's what we set out to do.'

He gestured disbelief. 'Oh, come on – you've got a clean slate. You've got prime position in the room. You've got it all!'

Her gaze softened; her eyes had not left his face for a second. 'Have I?' she said quietly.

Blood pounded in his ears; suddenly blankness, exhaustion, all thoughts of ending were a million miles away. He swung himself into the seat beside her and slammed the door shut.

'Haven't you?' he said.

Her smile broadened as she turned to the instrument panel. 'Did you get your altimeter fixed?'

He nodded. 'As a matter of fact, I did. Why? Where are you taking me?'

'Oh, I thought we could slip away. I know a quiet place nearby where we could have some dinner, maybe drink a little more than we should.' She looked at him archly. 'What do you say?'

'Where is this place?'

'France.'

He burst out laughing. 'It's hardly nearby.'

'It's twenty minutes, I promise you.' Gazing into his eyes, her face seemed incandescent, burning with more beauty, more passion, more sheer, enticing mystery, than he could see the end of in half a dozen years of gainful unemployment.

'Why not?' he said.